needing the next-door neighbor

a sweet romantic comedy

kristin canary

To the bookstagrammers who have been with me from the very beginning. You know who you are. I love you and couldn't do this without you. Thank you for your love and support, friends.

prologue

. . .

DON'T GET ME WRONG. I love my sister Alexis, and I am super happy for her right now.

But if I have to watch her kiss her new boyfriend Dax one more time today, I think I might scream. Is this how she felt being around Brooks and me for the last two years?

Who am I kidding? Brooks never looked at me like Dax looks at her—like he's freaking privileged just to know her, much less be dating her.

When Dax—from Alexis's couch—asks if she got him a piece of pumpkin pie, Alexis rolls her eyes from the kitchen, where half of her friends are dishing up Friends-giving Day dessert for their fiancés and the other half are waiting in the living room for their husbands to bring them some.

Then there's me, inching closer to the front door with my phone in my pocket and a plate of pie I got for me, myself, and I. Just Kennedy Matkin. Nobody to be responsible for me. Nobody to be responsible for.

My eyes burn. Ugh, so annoying. I do not want to cry over that jerk Brooks ever again, but does my stupid body listen to me? Nooooo, it just goes on leaking tears for a guy who has already moved on, if his Instagram account can be believed.

Which is why I have to make this phone call. I can't trespass on my sister's goodwill and kindness for too long.

I reach for the front door handle just as Alexis waltzes in with a plate and plops onto Dax's lap. He sets his chin on her shoulder. "For me?"

She forks a piece and holds it close to his lips. When he goes to bite it, she zooms it into her own mouth instead, groans. "Connor! This pie is amazing."

Dax says something low and throaty in her ear, and her eyes light up. "Dare," she says.

Oh, those two. They're impossibly adorable. I hope they get married and provide me with dozens of adorable nieces and nephews. But right now, it hurts my insides to see all these happy couples, so I open the door and duck out into the nippy November afternoon. I've been in San Diego for nearly two weeks and haven't really spent much time outside.

The porch is small but covered and a bit raised off the ground given that Alexis and her friends Shelby and Lauren live in a hilly neighborhood. Setting my pie down on the porch railing, I zip up my white Burberry jacket, a gift from my super-rich maternal grandma for my twenty-second birthday. (That was before I moved in with Brooks. For my twenty-third, she sent me a bridal catalog—a not-so-subtle hint that showed her traditional roots.)

Then I slip into one of the two white wicker chairs with faded floral pads and pull the plate onto my lap. It's going to serve as delicious fortitude before I make the dreaded call.

I breathe in, let my shoulders settle. Finally. Peace and—

Nails clatter up the porch steps and all I see is a black face and a flash of white teeth before there's a huge dog leaping up at me. "Ah!" I scream, crossing my arms and lifting them in the air to shield myself. "I'll give you anything, just don't take my face."

"Finley!" There's a sharp whistle and the dog's head goes up. "Where are you, boy?"

"Over here!" I shift as I call, and my plate—and the pie along with it—falls to the wooden porch floor. The chocolate lab begins happily eating, its huge tail knocking into me.

"Excuse me, sir." I cross my arms over my chest. "That's my pie you're eating."

Someone groans to the left of me. "Finley."

My head jerks that way and I freeze. *Hello, Hottie McScottie.* The most delicious man I've ever seen is approaching the porch. And I live in San Francisco, where there are lots of handsome men. But he's not attractive in the way that a lot of those city dwellers are —sculpted and waxed, with crisp suits and a dry martini in hand.

No, he's like that casual sort of effortlessly handsome, with simple low-slung jeans that are nice and worn, and a red Oklahoma University hoodie. I can tell he's quite fit thanks to the strain of the cotton fabric. And his blond curls next to tan skin? Mmm, my personal Kryptonite. (In case you were wondering, no, Brooks isn't blond at all. He's got a dark, brooding brow and pale skin, like a vampire without the sparkles.)

"I'm so sorry." The man sticks his hand through the porch railing and grabs the dog's collar. "Finley, that's not yours." His sentences are colored with a light Southern flare.

"At this point, you might as well let him finish it."

"He's normally so well-behaved, but he's still a puppy. A big one, but only a year old and—" His eyes flit to me, back to the dog. Then zero in on me again. "You don't live here."

I raise an eyebrow, push my hair behind an ear. "My sister owns the house and I'm staying … a while." Right now, Alexis and I are sharing her room, her bed. It's been nice to have a place to retreat to, and I haven't really decided what I'm doing. I figure if she's okay with it, maybe I'll stay through the holidays at the very least.

Of course, I need money to do even that. I like social media influencing, but it doesn't pay all the bills, especially in California. A flash of heat sears through me at the thought that I spent so much money—all of my inheritance from my dad—on my life with Brooks. And with him spreading nasty rumors about me, my online credibility has started taking a hit. I've somehow got to turn this around.

Alexis may think she should be taking care of me, but I've been taking care of myself my whole life. I'm not going to mooch off of her.

But that's a problem for another moment. Not this one. "I'm Kennedy."

"Oh." The man's light blue eyes keep holding onto me. I notice crinkles around the corners, like maybe he smiles a lot. I'd clock his age about early to mid-thirties —so, like Alexis and her friends, about a decade older than me. "I'm Ryan Rosche. The neighbor." With his free hand, he points to the house to our left.

"Ah! The hot doctor neighbor who runs around without his shirt on? I've heard a lot about you."

A deep flush spreads all the way up to his cheeks. "I don't know about that." He rubs a hand over his neck, and I get the distinct feeling he's uncomfortable. Fascinating. But what does he expect with a house full of women and a body like the one I suspect is lurking under his clothing? "I mean, yeah. I'm a doctor. And a neighbor. And I do run a lot. But …"

"The hot part?"

"Yeah. I don't know about that."

"Well, I'm a very objective third party, and I can confirm the truth of that statement. And I haven't even seen you without a shirt on."

He coughs. "Um."

I kind of want to giggle at his old-man modesty. Most guys who look like him would be strutting all around the yard crowing like a rooster about now. Leaning down, I pick up the plate that's been licked clean of crumbs thanks to young Finley here. Now that

Ryan's mentioned it, the dog's paws do look slightly too big for his body in that goofy teenage way both dogs and kids have.

"Do you want to join us for Friends-giving?" I ask.

"What now?"

"My sister and her friends. They do it every year." We spent yesterday—actual Thanksgiving—with Dax's family. "Everyone brought over their leftovers to share. Come on. There's plenty."

"Oh, thank you, but I've got company coming over." A small black car pulls up to his driveway. "I should head back." He lets go of Finley's collar, and the dog sits upright as a young girl and a beautiful, model-thin blonde woman climb from the car. With a bark, Finley bolts from the porch and the little girl squeals, dropping to her knees only to be tackled by the dog. Clearly they are well acquainted.

"Anyway. Sorry about the pie." Ryan scratches the back of his head. "And thanks for the invite. Tell everyone I say happy holidays."

"No problem. I will."

"Ryan!" the woman calls, waving—probably wondering who in the world he's talking to.

"Be right there." He turns to me, catches my gaze again. "Nice meeting you, Kennedy. Maybe I'll see you around."

Oh, goodness, I hope so. Nothing like a hot doctor to take one's mind off of no-good exes. "Mmm hmm," I say brilliantly.

He smiles and something shifts inside of me. Then he turns and heads toward the people waiting, including the woman whose head is tilted in my direction. Upon closer inspection, she looks a bit haggard and ducks back into the car to say something. After a bit, a teenage girl with Air Pods and a cell phone gets out.

Can't be a wife and kids, with the way he called them "company." Maybe a girlfriend? Ryan gives them all hugs and, arm around the woman's shoulders, guides the group inside.

Le sigh. Why are all the hot decent men taken?

A breeze kicks up, rustling some dead leaves that have fallen from a tree in Alexis's front yard. I've stalled long enough. Pulling my phone from my coat pocket, I start to dial.

When my grandmother answers, I push on a smile because even though we're not video chatting, she'll know if I'm frowning. Says she can hear it in people's voices. And she's an amazing businesswoman who's had huge success, so I don't doubt it.

"Well, finally deigning to call me, are we?"

Ugh. "Hi, Gran. Happy Thanksgiving."

"A day late."

"Right. Yeah. Sorry about that." I add a little fake cheerleader pep to my voice and remember that she is always a fan of getting straight to the point. "I'd like to talk to you about my trust fund."

one

. . .

Two Months Later

SO THIS IS MY LIFE—SERVING lattes to teens who think they're better than me because they've got Daddy's credit card and the latest Dolce & Gabbana purse.

"I'm sorry, you want a what?" I tuck a piece of hair behind my ear and lean in. It's possible with the whirring of the grinder behind me and the chatter from patrons at other tables that I misheard the girl, who can't be more than twelve despite her midriff-baring purple shirt and tight jeans.

Not that I can judge. I also grew up way too fast.

The girl turns to her carbon copy friend and they both roll their eyes before she redirects her attention to me. "I said, I want a 20/20."

Okay, I might be fairly new to barista-ing at Java Awakening—an adorable San Diego coffee shop my sister Alexis and her friends frequent—but I still consider myself in the know about all things coffee.

"Oh, that must be new!" I snatch up a to-go cup and a Sharpie. "What's in it?"

"OMG, can you believe this lady?" the girl stage whispers to her friend.

Then, like I'm super old and hard of hearing, she says—nice and slow AND loud—"It's a latte with twenty pumps of vanilla and twenty pumps of hazelnut, whole milk, whip, and caramel drizzle." She smacks her gum and twirls her sleek black hair that's quite obviously been professionally cut and colored.

Must be nice. Over the last few months, the highlights in my brown hair have grown out, and its split ends hang past the spot just below my shoulders where I prefer it. But that's what happens when you're suddenly poor.

"Hey lady, you listening?"

I jump at her snappy attitude—and fingers. Oh my sheesh, I really, really want to say something sarcastic back to her. My manager Josh's wife Kayla probably would. I've seen her take people down a notch or two a few times. But I can't afford to lose the one source of income I have at the moment. Not that Josh would fire me. I don't think.

"Of course." Showing her the writing on the cup, I quirk an eyebrow.

"Fine. But make sure it's 190 degrees exactly or I'm asking for a refund." Little Miss Attitude glances down at her phone and starts furiously typing as if it isn't the rudest thing in the world.

But maybe nobody's ever taught her as much. Maybe she's just copying what she knows. A product of her environment. This mean girl, who is probably at the top of the food chain at her school, is most likely this way because she's trying to prove something. Or she's scared. Or unsure of who she is.

Or all of the above.

I know because I've been that girl. Not *mean*, per se, but putting on an act for the world to see. And for a long time, it served me well. Once upon a time, not so very long ago, I was the one with a closet full of new and expensive clothes, for whom restaurants and hotels comped meals and stays, just for a mere mention in my social media posts.

I had it all—until I didn't.

Now I'm here, aged twenty-three, sharing a small bedroom with my sister, working and saving to go back to college—which, at this point, won't happen for several years unless I can miraculously find another job that pays more than minimum wage. Alexis has offered to pay my way, but she's already done too much for me. So, unless Gran decides to release my trust fund, I'm doing this on my own.

Which is good. Because I've got to show everyone— myself included—that I can.

Way to be a bummer, Kennedy. Shrugging away my too-dreary thoughts, I flourish Little Miss Attitude's order onto a cup with the marker. "That'll be six-fifty-nine."

She hands me her daddy's credit card, and when I flash her a determined smile, you'd think I threatened her dog. Her narrowed eyes are proof that apparently she isn't used to people being nice in response to her sourness.

After her friend orders a 20/20 as well, they move aside, and I head for the espresso machine, where Josh Gregory is currently finishing up an order of his own. I respect that he's the kind of manager who gets his hands dirty and doesn't just boss us all around from on high. When I come into his periphery, he flashes me a tired smile. "How's it going, Kennedy?"

"Just another Wednesday in paradise."

He chuckles, but ironically, I think he believes this *is* paradise. His uncle owns the coffee shop from afar, and Josh loves nurturing the space. While many guys would want to climb corporate ladders, he's content with his life. And why shouldn't he be? He's got a brand-new baby girl and an intelligent, smoking-hot wife who quite literally can't keep her hands off of him.

"Well, thanks again for covering extra hours so I could take some paternity leave." Josh pushes his thick glasses farther up on his nose and lets loose a yawn. "Kayla and I appreciated knowing you and the others had things under control those few weeks I was out." He collects his three drinks and handles them like a pro, not spilling a drop. But then he just stands there, blinking, like he forgot what he's supposed to do with them.

"No problem at all. Just let me know if you still need some extra coverage." I cock my head, smile. "Seems you could use the rest."

And I could use the money. Being a barista is actually kind of fun—it reminds me a little bit of waitressing at the high-end bar where I worked briefly before meeting Brooks in San Francisco a few years ago—but it pays absolute beans (no pun intended), especially when I can only get twenty hours in a normal week.

If I ever hope to rebuild my life, to save enough to resume college, to eventually get a degree that qualifies me for a job that pays actual money to live on, I definitely need to get another job now—either a full-time one or something else that's part-time, like the retail job I worked over the holidays.

Of course, I could always take the position Gran offered me two months ago. But I have my reasons for saying no. Not reasons that Marsha Montgomery understands. But reasons that are all mine.

"Thanks." Josh nods as he balances the drinks in his hands against his long-sleeved *Star Wars* T-shirt. "I'll keep your offer in mind. Rey still hasn't gotten her days and nights straight."

"I've heard that's pretty common." In fact, Evie Bryant—who, along with Kayla, used to live in Alexis's house before she got married—said the same thing. She had little baby Fitz on January fifth, just ten days before Kayla gave birth to Rey. (And yes, they both named their babies after fictional characters: Fitzwilliam Darcy from *Pride & Prejudice* and Rey from the newest round of *Star Wars* films.)

While Josh serves his drinks to the waiting customers, I crank out the two "20/20s" and then deliver them with all the chipper spunk I can manage. My life may be lame, but I've dealt with a lot worse things than snarky teen girls in my twenty-three years, and it costs me nothing to be nice to them. Who knows?

Maybe it'll remind them they are more than the things they pretend to be. Maybe I can perform a little tiny miracle and brighten their day.

Little Miss Attitude snatches her drink, takes a sip. Frowns. Wrinkles her nose. "Ugh."

Her friend does the same. "Double ugh."

They both tighten their grip on their purse straps, flip their hair over their shoulders, and flounce from the coffee shop into the cloudy California afternoon.

Welp. A miracle maker, I am not.

With a sigh, I move back to the register and take the next order. For the next few hours, there's a steady stream of customers, including Kayla and Rey, who surprise Josh with a visit. Despite having just had a baby a few weeks ago, the woman is gorgeous with her long torso and brown hair that's pulled back in a pony-tail—albeit with something white and crusty that is quite possibly dried spit-up or old milk in her bangs.

She comes behind the counter and steps up to give Josh a kiss, and I don't miss how her hand darts around to his backside and squeezes his butt. He kisses her back, then leans down to nuzzle the sleeping baby in the stroller before attending to the lone customer in line at the moment.

"And there's Kennedy, our lifesaver!" Kayla turns to me and leans in for a quick hug. I don't know why this still takes me by surprise. Even though she's Alexis's friend, not mine, all of them—Kayla, Evie, Shelby, Lauren, and Alexis—have welcomed my extended stay here with open arms. Still, I never want to make assumptions about where I stand.

Where I belong.

I mean, I know Alexis and I are bonded forever, even if she's just my half-sister. Our dad died in a plane accident when I was just four years old. That's when Alexis discovered her father had another family—my mom Pippa and me. But instead of turning away from me, hating me, she claimed me. Loved me in spite of it all.

And I'll never be able to repay her for that.

Now that Mom's been gone for five years, the only people I really have are Alexis and Gran. One loves me unconditionally. The other … well, let's just say she's undecided about me at the moment.

Who am I kidding? She's been undecided about me from the moment I was born. To her, I'm just Pippa 2.0.

A disgrace to the Montgomery name.

I pull back from Kayla and glance down at Rey, whose dark curls match Josh's and whose perfect little nose is a replica of Kayla's. She is absolute perfection, not because of her looks, but because she was the product of true love. A love that gives and sacrifices and constantly chooses each other.

Someday, I hope Rey knows how lucky she is.

I touch her soft cheek. "She's amazing."

"She is—even when she bites my boobs and makes sure I don't sleep a wink."

Looking up, I expect Kayla to wear a joking expression. But she's completely serious.

"That sounds … kind of awful."

She sighs. "And equally wonderful. Such is motherhood."

"Hmm." My fingers find the small gold cross necklace at my throat—the one my mom gave me for my eighteenth birthday just before she died from a quick bout with cancer. "Well, it's good to see you out and about."

"I was absolutely dying being shut away in that house alone—well, you know what I mean. Without adult interaction." Kayla squeezes my elbow. "Josh told me we could go out to dinner after closing."

I check my watch. "That's not that far off. I can cover the rest of the shift alone if you want to take off now."

"Really?" Kayla throws her arms around me again—in an almost desperate way—and I catch a faint whiff of baby powder and soap. "You're the best. Although actually, if you'd like to join us, you are more than welcome. I have a text out to the gang to see if anyone else can meet up. I think Shelby and Eric have a late meeting or something at the school, but Evie's ready to rejoin the land of the living again too. Want to come?"

"Oh, that's really nice." But how do I say that I just can't deal with the noise tonight? And what's wrong with me? I used to live for the party scene, the social interactions. Lately though, the perfect evening consists of a glass of wine and binging old episodes of *The Bachelor*. "I think Chloe and I were going to hang out at the house, though."

Hopefully Chloe won't mind me using her as an excuse. The current princess—yeah, you heard me … a real live princess—of Kentonia and her bodyguard Tia are crashing at Alexis's house so she can spend time with her future sister-in-law Lauren and "escape her royal duties for a while." She's the other "outsider" in the group, though you wouldn't know it with her vivacious personality and flawless style. But it's been nice to not feel like the only one in "the gang" who isn't an original housemate.

Frowning, Kayla pulls her phone from the diaper bag hanging from the stroller handle. "I thought Chloe was coming to dinner with us."

"Really? That's odd." If that's true, then I actually might have the house to myself tonight—a rarity. "I'll text her and see what's up." I should probably just be honest with Kayla. Hopefully it doesn't make her think less of me. "I'm pretty zonked today too. Think I need some quiet time at home."

She studies me for a while. "You doing okay?"

My fingers itch at the scrutiny and I move toward the sink to wash up some dishes. "Asks the woman who just gave birth." Grabbing a huge smoothie pitcher, I dunk it into the soap suds.

"I can still tell when someone else is having a rough day. You thinking about your no-good ex?"

"Yes. And no. It's just"—I use a long-handled scrubber to nudge out a stuck piece of frozen fruit from beneath the blender's blade at the bottom—"everything."

"Still trying to figure out where you belong?"

Dang. Is this woman a mind reader? "Something like that." Because not only do I need to figure out my future —where I want to live, what I want to do, where I want to go to school, who I want to be—but I need to do it all in such a way that the family I have left is proud of me. Alexis has provided a safe space for the last few months, but she and Dax are getting more serious. She's gone half the time to visit him in Los Angeles.

She knows me better than anyone else, but I'm the only one who can create a real future for myself.

No pressure, right?

I scrub harder and, once the fruit piece comes free, rinse it and the soap down the empty side of the sink.

"Let me tell you something I had to learn the hard way, okay, Ken?" Kayla uses my nickname effortlessly, like she actually knows me—not just the me I project out to the world, but the real me. Then again, she's a dating coach for a living, so she's probably used to dealing with hot messes like me. "You belong with the people who love you for who you are—and they won't leave. So rely on them." She pauses. "On us."

Okay, well, that was unexpected. And beautiful. I set the clean but wet blender upside down on the drying rack. Glance over at her. "Thanks, Kayla."

"You got it, girlfriend." A tiny, fussing coo rises from the stroller. In seconds, it becomes a wail. "And that's my cue to feed my baby." She grabs the stroller handles and begins to maneuver it toward the kitchen, likely headed to Josh's office in the back. "Feel free to come to dinner when you get off if you change your mind. I'll text you the location once we decide where we're going."

"I will. Thanks."

She disappears, and a half hour later, the little family of three is out the main door. I serve a handful of new customers, clean up the machines, and politely usher out a few stragglers. After I lock up, I hustle against the cold air for my car—a beat-up yellow Toyota that once belonged to my mom. When I climb inside, I start it up and relish the heat pumping from the vents. San Diego's temps might be temperate, but the evenings can still get chilly with the wind coming off the Pacific.

My phone buzzes in my purse. I reach for it and groan when I see a text from Gran—a picture of a gorgeous office overlooking the San Francisco bay. And a note: *A life of respectability awaits you once you've decided to dry your eyes and act like a Montgomery.*

Just like I do with all of her texts lately—one or two a week with messages that are just as passive-aggressive—I ignore this one and lock my phone. Then I turn on the radio and blare 'N Sync, an old-school boy band that Lauren and Chloe tell me I've just gotta try.

I somewhat see the appeal as I race down the freeway to *Pop*.

Sure, I might be single and broke and sharing a queen-sized bed with my older sister who thinks she has to take care of me, but at least here, I'm free. Brooks wasn't what I would call abusive, but he also didn't give me space to be me.

And I didn't demand it, either. I was too afraid to lose him.

Then I did.

But I don't regret it. I don't miss him. Being here has given me the time and perspective I need to see what an unhealthy relationship it was.

I head toward Point Loma and before I know it, I'm back at Alexis's house. Nobody else's car is in the driveway—so I really *do* have the rare night at home alone.

It sounds completely glorious. Does that make me totally lame?

Hauling myself and my stuff out of the car, I head to the darkened front porch. Canned laughter drifts from the windows of the house next door—the house where the hottest doctor known to man lives. Dr. Ryan Rosche, who I've only spoken to once a few months ago but have waved casually to now and again when we're both coming and going … or when he's in his backyard throwing a ball to his black Labrador Finley … or when he's leaving for a shirtless run around the neighborhood and I happen to drive past … slowly.

Still, more than just being handsome, his best feature is his kind smile. Of course, he doesn't only use it on me. He also uses it on the woman I assume is his girl-friend and her daughters. I've also seen them coming and going quite frequently.

Which means that the guy is clearly off-limits. Because I'm not a man stealer. Not like Mom. Alexis claims that Pippa didn't know my dad was married with a kid when she got with him, but I honestly have my doubts.

Still, whenever I *do* get back into the dating game, I want it to be with a guy like Ryan—genuine, friendly, and caring. Someone whose smile makes the world a better place. Who cares about more than his number of social media followers and his bank account.

So, basically, the opposite of Brooks Marsden.

"Okay, Kennedy, stop being weird and go inside."

Yes, I talk to myself sometimes, all right? Thankfully nobody is here to witness my insanity.

I shove open the front door—and nearly scream at the sight of someone sitting on our couch.

Guess I'm not alone after all.

two

I BLINK INTO THE DARKNESS, the only light from inside emanating from my intruder's cell phone.

Weapon. I should get a weapon. Or, you know, call the police. But what if it's one of my roommates and for some reason, her car isn't here? There are many good explanations for what could be going on.

There could also be a murderer on Alexis's bright blue couch.

Biting my lip, I make a decision and reach into my purse for my keychain. Thanks to my experiences with my mom and her string of boyfriends growing up, I learned a thing or two about self-protection. On my thirteenth birthday, I bought myself a cute and clippable can of Mace, and I've replaced it every few years since.

Might finally be time to use it.

Taking the can of Mace in hand, I step forward. The door hinges squeak because apparently I'm the unstealthiest person in the history of stealth.

The intruder's phone lowers and a tinny voice whispers, "Hello?"

Wait. Straightening, I flick on the light.

Okay, unless there's a petite young murderer going around the neighborhood targeting the people next door, I think I'm safe. Because on my couch is a wisp of a blonde-haired girl—one I recognize. She's the older daughter of the woman I assume to be Dr. Ryan's girlfriend. I've always thought she was maybe fourteen or so, but upon closer inspection, I realize she must be closer to eleven.

But that's not the point.

What in the world is she doing *here*?

Lowering my Mace and tossing my keys back into my purse, I step fully into the living room and shut the door behind me. "Hey." I try to say it super casually so the girl doesn't bolt. Then I hang up my purse, remove my coat and hang that too, and slip off my wedges as if I have all the time in the world.

Meanwhile, the girl watches my every move, her whole body tense and ready to spring off the couch that, to my knowledge, she's never sat on before. So instead of sitting beside her, I lower myself onto the patchwork overstuffed chair on the other side of the room and pull my feet up under my body. "What's up?"

Mascara streaks down her cheeks. It looks mostly dried, and she'd likely be horrified if she knew a virtual stranger was seeing her like this. I mean, I would have been when I was her age. But despite her makeup debacle, she's a pretty girl. Her hair isn't professionally styled, but it's thick and luxurious, the kind I can only dream of, and the rest of her makeup looks natural. Her clothes are stylish—a soft-looking, cable-knit turtleneck, black leggings, and boots that look like Doc Martens but I can tell at a glance are off-brand.

I really, really want to ask what she's doing here. And also, if Ryan and her mom know she's here. But I also don't want her to run off.

She bites her lip. Blinks at me before her gaze darts back to her phone, then finds me again. The girl opens her mouth to say something, but shuts it just as quickly.

Looks like it's up to me to carry this conversation. "I'm Kennedy, by the way. What's your name?"

"Ava."

Okay. This is good. Progress. "My sister Alexis owns this house, and I've been here the last few months." I pause. No reaction. Just a stare. "I've seen you visiting Ryan with your mom and sister."

There. A flinch of emotion scurries across Ava's eyes, her lips. She turns her head away, toward the window. "My mom dumped us here last week."

Her language does not imply that this is a good thing, and yet I keep an upbeat tone. "I'm sure you miss her. When does she get back from her trip?"

Instead of sinking farther into the couch, the girl sits up straighter, spearing with me a glare and lifting her chin. "Don't you care that I broke into your house?"

I glance at the back door. No damage that I can see. And the front doorknob certainly wasn't broken. "Did you?"

Ava huffs. "Well, no. The back door was unlocked."

Really? Yikes. I'll have to talk with the girls about

that. "Okay. Well, just so you know, I'm not mad that you're here."

"You … aren't?"

The way her lip trembles ever so slightly makes me want to leap from this chair and gather her into a hug. There's a lot going on beneath the surface with Ava—and something in me wants to protect her from it. Maybe it's just because I didn't have anyone protecting me for so much of my life. Not until Alexis moved out to California after she graduated high school. Even then, I lived with Mom. Not that she was a completely horrible mother, but … yeah. Alexis could only protect me from so much.

"Nope. But I do wonder if Ryan might be worried about you?" I run my fingers over the tassels on the throw pillow sitting beside me. "Because I'm guessing he doesn't know you're here?"

It takes her a minute, but she eventually picks up her phone and starts swiping at the screen. "I dunno. We were watching some stupid kid show and he fell asleep when he got home from work. And … I just needed some air."

Asleep at seven-thirty on a Thursday? Maybe he had an early shift. "Then what happened?"

"You don't even know me. Why do you care?"

Uh, because you're in my sister's house. That's what I want to say. But I know that's not what she needs to hear. "Who says we're only allowed to care about people we know?" I get up slowly and move to the couch, being sure to leave a couch cushion between us. The sweet scent of peaches surrounds me, the same shampoo scent I chose when I was her age. That thought makes me smile. "Can I ask you a question?"

Still not looking at me, Ava shrugs. I'm taking that as a yes.

"Why *are* you here? And remember—I'm not mad."

Her thumb jabs something on the screen. I peek and see she's playing Candy Crush. One of my faves when I don't want to face reality too. "It was cold outside but I didn't want to go back in."

Warning bells go off in my brain. Why didn't she want to return to Ryan's house? Ryan doesn't immediately strike me as the type to be abusive, but sometimes the biggest predators appear to be the nicest guys. I edge forward on my seat. "Does Ryan ... does he hurt you?"

"What? No!" Dropping her phone into her lap, she crosses her arms, her face twisted in a horrified expression. "He would never hurt Mila or me."

Mila. Must be the younger sister, who I'd clock around four or five years.

Inhaling, I focus on her chin—her brave chin that's doing its best to be unaffected, grown-up—but is giving itself away with the occasional tremor. "This is a safe space. So if someone really *is* hurting you—"

"Seriously. He's not hurting me. Mind your own business."

"Okay." I hold up my hands. "It's just that I've been around a lot of mean guys in my life, and I want to make sure you're safe."

Phone in her fist, Ava stands. "Ugh, I just wanted a little peace and quiet, okay? Is that a crime?"

Hearing that walking into our house without invitation actually *might* be considered a crime probably won't help diffuse the situation, so I stand too and take a step back. "Totally understandable. But hey. No harm, no foul."

"Great." Without another word, she turns to leave.

I scurry after her, not bothering to slip on my coat or shoes, and exit the house. An owl hoots somewhere in the distance and a white car drives past, its tire crunching gravel that's scattered across the asphalt, its headlights temporarily casting our shadows onto the sidewalk.

Ava crosses the space between the houses and looks back at me. "What are you doing?"

"Coming with you."

"I can get home on my own."

"I know that, but I need to talk to Ryan about this."

"I'll just slip inside." Her eyebrows narrow together into a unibrow. "He doesn't need to know."

How many times did I think that about my mom growing up? *She doesn't need to know.* Half the time, I was the more responsible person in our two-woman show. But Ava shouldn't have to carry any burdens—which lying always ends up being. "Sorry, babe. I'll come with you and talk to him, okay? Make sure he knows you weren't a bother at all. But he does need to know." *Just in case it happens again …*

A frustrated growl is all the response I get and then Ava is heading for Ryan's front door. Without knocking, she goes inside, the door slamming behind her.

Okay, then. Guessing I don't rank at the top of Ava's

list of favorite people right now. Oh, how I wish I could just brush this aside, be the cool neighbor who lets her sneak out and do her own thing.

Adulting is for the birds.

But I know this is what's ultimately best for her. Honestly, it's what I wish someone had cared enough to do for me in my rebellious teen years whenever Alexis wasn't around.

Gritting my teeth against the inevitable, I knock and wait. When there isn't an answer, I push open the door to find a formal dining room turned game room, complete with foosball and pool tables, and I'm met with a variety of delicious scents. Ryan's home is maple syrup mixed with a hint of bonfire—that woodsy, earthy smell that can only mean a man lives here.

A good-smelling man.

I shiver, then scold my unconscious reaction. *He's taken, remember, Kennedy?*

Ava is nowhere to be found, but my knock has apparently aroused at least one member of the family. Ryan's dog Finley is standing alert and growling from a dog bed in the corner.

"Hey, bud. It's me. Kennedy. The nice lady who gave you pumpkin pie a few months ago." Fine. *Gave* is kind of generous considering he basically tackled me on Alexis's front porch before stealing my dessert.

He cocks his head, but I can't tell if he recognizes me or not. His eyes follow me as I inch my way toward the archway that leads to the next room over, where a TV is blaring.

Then, giving a bark, Finley races toward me.

Does the tongue lolling out of his mouth mean he's happily chasing me or sizing me up for dinner? I *am* an intruder after all. Either way, I can just picture his one-hundred-something frame flinging me across the room like a rag doll.

Yeah, nope. I'm not taking the time to find out what his intentions are.

My feet pound the tile floor as I round the corner, glimpsing a mounted TV with credits from some movie rolling. Gah. It's semi-dark with only a few lights on, but a quick survey of the room doesn't turn up anyone who can call off the hound about to tackle me. Then my gaze zeroes in on a couch with a high back.

Bingo. The perfect place to get out of the mutt's path. Jumping it will at least put a large obstacle between us.

So, channeling a freaking Olympic pole vaulter, I place one hand on the back of the couch and fling my whole body up, head swiveling back to keep track of the dog.

My intention is to tuck my body and land facedown on the soft couch, then roll off and keep running if I must.

Instead, I fall headlong into a hard chest.

"Oof."

I don't know if it's me or the man I just tackled who says it—maybe both—but despite the wind that's been knocked out of me, I am amply distracted by a pair of strong arms that wind their way around my waist.

"Kennedy?"

Gathering my courage, I open my eyes and stare down into Dr. Ryan's.

Dr. Ryan, who was clearly napping on his couch until he was very rudely awakened.

Dr. Ryan, who is blinking up at me.

Dr. Ryan, who has … pink and purple barrettes in his blond curls?

And I know this is awkward. I know this is bad. But I can't help myself. "Who's your stylist? I definitely have to meet her."

"What?" One of Ryan's hands leaves my back to feel his hair. He groans, and his fingers fall back into place. "I must have fallen asleep. And Mila took advantage." His Southern accent hints of teasing. "How do I look?"

I resist the urge to touch his hair because *boundaries*. But I can't help the smile that slips onto my lips. "Marvelous, dah-ling."

A giggle floats from across the room and I swivel my head to find a little pixie in a Tinkerbell costume sitting in a large chair that simply swallows her. She's brushing a Barbie's brown hair. "Hi."

"Well, hello there. Do you happen to be Mila, the famous hair stylist I've heard so much about?"

"That's me!" She uses her Barbie's arm to wave at me, and oh my goodness, she's the cutest thing, with her tangled blonde curls that hang down her back and smudges of chocolate on her face. I find the source of the chocolate easily—a bowl on the black coffee table filled with M&Ms. The bowl is accompanied by an empty pizza box, several dirty cups and plates, and some small piles of what looks like kinetic sand. In fact, the whole room is kind of a disaster. It looks like a toy store exploded.

"You're one of the ladies from next door," Mila states matter-of-factly.

"I am. My name's Kennedy."

"Can I do your hair next? Barbies aren't as fun as real people."

"Of course you can. But maybe not tonight, since it's almost bedtime."

Mila tilts her head, considering my response before nodding. Then, "Why are you hugging Uncle Ryan like that? Are you his girlfriend?"

Gah. Right. "Um, no. I just … fell." I attempt to push myself upright, but realize too late that means I'm fondling his chest. Not that it isn't a nice chest …

Kennedy, the man has a girlfr—

But wait. "*Uncle* Ryan?" Does that mean that the woman I've been assuming is his girlfriend is actually a sister or sister-in-law?

My heart does a little jig. *Settle down in there.*

"Yes." Ryan clears his throat and looks down at my hands splayed across his pecs.

Kill me now. "Sorry," I murmur, moving my hands to the couch cushion on either side of him. But because his arms are still wound around my waist, I meet resistance when I push—and fall back toward him. He grunts and loosens his grip, allowing me the freedom to slip off the couch and stand. I wind one arm around my waist and one up into my hair. "Well, that was awkward."

"Was it?" Chuckling, he sits up and leans forward, elbows on his knees. He's still wearing green scrubs, and whew, how I love a man in uniform.

But that's not what I should be thinking about. Instead, I should be trying to explain why I jumped and subsequently groped a sleeping man. "Um, I don't normally go couch diving, but your dog was—" At that moment, the menace trots toward me as calm as can be, sits, and stares up at me with huge innocent eyes.

So that's how it's gonna be, huh, traitor?

A tiny grin flicks over Ryan's lips as he takes the both of us in. "My dog was ...?" His eyes study me, and I get lost in the sea of blue. *Seriously? Sea of blue. How corny are you?*

"He was chasing me like I was the freaking mailman and he hadn't eaten in days, okay?" With a laugh, I shake my head before finally giving into Finley and patting his head. His fur is surprisingly soft. "See? I'll pet you if you don't charge at me like a maniac."

"Like I told you before, he's still a puppy. Though I can't blame him for chasing a pretty woman, can you, Mila?"

The stars outside have nothing on her big smile. "Nope."

Eek. Okay, no big deal. The hot neighbor—who it turns out might be single—thinks I'm pretty. No. Big. Deal.

Oh my sheesh. When did I become so desperate for a man's attention? I used to have thousands of hot guys sliding into my DMs and commenting about how gorgeous I was. (And not just those creeper fake accounts that are a random guy's name and four or five numbers on the end. Legit guys from legit accounts.)

But this … it's definitely different. Still, I'm not going to read too much into it.

"So, you're probably wondering why I'm here."

"The thought *had* occurred to me once or twice." He stands and heads toward Mila, who is still focused on her doll's hair. Then he squats beside her. "Hey, Pumpkin. Time for bed, okay? You have preschool tomorrow." He rubs his hand down her hair in the gentlest manner. It takes absolutely no time at all to see that this man loves this little girl. Even though he's just her uncle—not her father—he's got the same look in his eyes that Josh does when he holds Baby Rey.

"No, I don't. I did today."

Ryan's shoulders stiffen and his hand pauses. But then he plays with the ends of her hair. "That's right. It's Wednesday, isn't it?"

"Mmm hmm. So tomorrow, you can stay home with me and bake cookies and then we can go to the park."

He groans. "I wish we could, but I already took off as much time as I could from work the last few weeks."

"So who's gonna stay with me now that Nanny Lois isn't coming back?"

Hmmm. I'm trying not to intrude—I really should just go—but the wheels are turning in my head trying to piece together what's going on. Ava said something about her mom dumping them here, right? I assumed she was on a short trip, but what if it's more than that?

And why did the nanny quit? Or maybe Mila's just misunderstood what's going on.

It's none of my business, really. I'm just here to tell Ryan about Ava sneaking into our house. And yet, I can't help but care. Especially when it seems Dr. Ryan might be in over his head.

"I'm not quite sure," Ryan says. "But I'll figure something out. Now come on. Say goodnight to Miss Kennedy."

It takes her a moment, but Mila reaches for his hand —so small in his—and gets up. Then, before I know what's happening, she races toward me and throws her arms around my thighs as she buries her head in my waist. "Night, Miss Kenny."

Gah. Can I keep her? I hug her back. "Goodnight, Miss Mila. I look forward to getting my hair done by you sometime very soon."

Her eyes pop up. "What about tomorrow? *You* could stay with me when Uncle Ryan goes to work."

"Mila." Ryan approaches quickly and peels his niece off of me. "I'm sure Miss Kennedy has things to do tomorrow."

"Actually, I work at a coffee shop but I'm off tomorrow." Smiling at Mila, I wink. "And I'd love to hang out with Miss Mila here. Though I can't promise the house won't burn down if we try to make cookies. I'm not much of a cook."

"Oh, I've made cookies with my mama lots of times. I'm a expert."

If only we all could have such confidence. "That would be fantastic."

"Are you … sure?" Ryan's forehead is adorably furrowed, and the way his hair is still bound in barrettes and sticking straight up only draws more attention to the fact. "I hate to put you out."

"It sounds like you need someone, and I only had plans to binge reality TV." I wave at Mila. "I'd much rather hang out with you." Then my gaze moves back to Ryan. "But let's talk after you put her down, okay? I'll wait here."

It takes him a long moment, but he finally blows out a breath and nods. "I'll be back in a few."

"No problem."

He and Mila head down the hall. I might as well make myself useful so after flicking on the rest of the lights and turning off the TV, I grab all of the trash and carry it to the kitchen, which is compact but still more spacious than Alexis's. It even has a small island, which is currently cluttered with dirty dishes.

By the time Ryan emerges thirty minutes later, his living room and kitchen are more spotless than my own room ever is. He stops mid-stride and looks around. "You did *not* have to do that."

I dry my hands on a dish towel and shrug before heading back toward the couch. Finley follows me. Apparently we're best buds now. "I didn't mind."

Ryan lowers himself onto the couch. "Sorry that took so long. She desperately needed a quick bath, and then asked for three books instead of the normal two."

"If she's like other kids, she'll probably pop out in search of a glass of water later," I tease as I drop onto the other end of the couch. "She's a doll."

"Yeah. She and Ava are both amazing kids." He stares at the now-clean coffee table and blinks. Sighs.

This poor guy is carrying the weight of something heavy on his shoulders. And I want to help carry it. Not because he's attractive—though he definitely is that—but because I know what it's like. The carrying things alone bit. Pretending to be strong when you're actually breaking inside.

"Um," I start.

His attention jolts toward me. Did he forget I was here?

My fingers smooth down my dark jeans. "So the reason I'm here in the first place is because I came home from work to find Ava in my sister's house."

"What?" Ryan's voice holds a panicked edge to it. "Are you serious? What was she doing there? Was she causing trouble? Was she … stealing things?"

"No, not at all. She was just sitting on my couch, scrolling on her phone." I shrug. "I think she just wanted a place to be alone and saw that nobody was home at our house."

"She has her own room here. She and Mila both do." He scrubs both of his hands up and down his face. "I'm so sorry. That wouldn't have happened if I hadn't fallen asleep. But I had to take a 24-hour shift and it was crazy busy, and then I got a call from the nanny, who I finally found after looking for two weeks, and she's quitting because apparently she's allergic to dogs and failed to tell me that in the three interviews we had together."

"Wow. That's … a lot."

"Tell me about it. I got off work early and jetted

home just in time for her to abandon ship. I ordered a pizza, and apparently, fell asleep on the job." Finally, he peeks up at me and freezes, his jaw ticking. "I'm sorry. I don't know why I just told you all of that. This isn't your problem."

"It's really fine. Actually, it's nice to hear about someone else's problems for once. I've been thinking about mine too much lately." I nudge his foot with my own. "How long are the girls here for?"

"Six months at least."

So long. "Where ..."

"Is my sister?" A pause. "Jail. She recently got a DUI and was finally sentenced a few weeks ago."

"For six months? That seems harsh." Then again, a DUI is no laughing matter.

"Yeah, well, Sophie's an addict and it wasn't her first offense, unfortunately."

Those poor girls. My mother was many things, but thankfully, an addict wasn't one of them. "And you're their next of kin? Isn't there anyone who can help you?"

He runs his fingers through his hair and stops at one of the barrettes. Maybe he forgot they were there. "No. My parents aren't here anymore." Ryan tries to unclip the barrette, but can't seem to figure it out. His fingers fumble until he finally huffs and gives up.

It would be kind of hilarious if he wasn't clearly struggling with other things. Taking pity on him, I scoot a tad bit closer. The cushion creaks beneath me. "Here." I motion for him to lean his head forward. "Let me help."

For a moment, he just stares at me, but eventually

inclines his head toward me. Then, "You're really willing to watch the girls tomorrow? I have to leave at seven. Ava takes the bus to school and has a key, but I hate for her to come home to an empty house. You probably notice she's a bit … difficult. But both of them are just feeling so abandoned." Another stretch of silence. "I'll pay you, of course."

I reach for the first barrette and unsnap it with ease, resisting the urge to run my fingers through the freed curl. Does this man realize he's got freaking beautiful hair? "I'm really willing. And the pay isn't necessary. I'm happy to help." Gently pulling loose another barrette and another, I pile them on my lap. "I have to work Friday morning from eight to one, or I'd offer to watch them that day too."

"Well, actually." He shakes his head. "Never mind."

"Tell me."

He peeks up at me, a flicker of blue under his lashes. Our faces are closer than I realized. "Mila has preschool on Mondays, Wednesdays, and Fridays until two. But I can't ask you—"

"Oh, perfect. I'll watch them that day too until you get home." Unsnapping the last barrette, I lower my hands. "All done."

He straightens, swallows. "Thank you, Kennedy."

Now my heart's jigging like it's a freaking river dance queen. "It was just a couple of barrettes." Gathering them in my hands, I hold them out toward him.

"No, not that. Well, yeah, that too. But just … thank you."

He accepts the barrettes, and his fingers brush mine. The touch is innocent—but electric.

I hold back a shiver. "It's my pleasure." And it is. Because when I think of those girls, all they've lost, I know I have no choice but to help. "That's what neighbors do."

three

· · ·

I DIDN'T KNOW LOOKING after a four-year-old all day and an eleven-year-old for part of the day could be so tiring.

"Miss Kenny!" Mila—a boundless cyclone of energy despite the fact she played at the park for two hours and didn't nap at all—races across the living room and flings herself onto my lap. "Can I do your hair now?"

Ooo, that sounds blessedly wonderful. I can sit still for that, right? But one glance at the clock on my phone nixes that idea. "I'm sorry, sweetness, but we have to go."

"Go where?"

"To the social worker's office, remember?" I'm not sure what exactly they have to do, but with the custody situation, there must be lots of hoops to jump through. "Uncle Ryan is meeting us there after work."

"Oh yeah! That lady's nice. She has lollipops." She

hops up and races around the coffee table, pumping her little arms in the air. "I get a lol-li-pop. Lol-li-pop."

I giggle at her antics and haul myself to my feet as well. Note to self: Wedges are not a solid shoe choice for entertaining a preschooler all day. I'll need to dig around in my half of Alexis's closet to find some flats or tennis shoes. "Okay, chop-chop. Head to your room and grab the clothes I laid out for you. You can change yourself, right?"

She's in the Tinkerbell dress again, and it's completely filthy. I assume it's machine washable, but I'll let Ryan deal with that later. Right now, the priority is getting the girls out the door and to their appointment on time. Hopefully I can finally coax Ava from her room. She came straight inside after getting off the bus and, without a word of greeting, went into her room.

"Of course I can, silly. I'm four and a half!" Mila veers from her path and heads down the hallway.

Finally, a moment of quiet. But I haven't minded the noise, not really. Mila has energy, but other than a few moments of stubborn willpower, she really was the sweetest little companion all day. Can't say the same about the preteen, but now's my chance to start making inroads with her.

I walk to Ava's room and knock on the white door. "Ava?"

No answer.

I try the handle and peek inside. Ava is lying on her bed, facedown, looking at her phone, earbuds in. She doesn't glance up at me until I advance inside and wave my hand between her face and the screen. Then she jerks upright and holds her phone to her chest, as if guarding state secrets. I smile and wave at her, making a motion from my ear down to indicate she should take out her earbud.

She does so, though it's at a sloth's pace. "What?"

"It's time to go to the social worker's."

"I'm not going."

I tilt my head. "Your uncle is meeting us there."

"You and Mila can go. I'm staying here." She crosses her arms, apparently an indication that she means business.

Ho boy. I don't envy the social worker, having to put up with this attitude. Of course, she's probably used to it. And maybe since she's had training—unlike me—she actually has the skills and knowledge to help Ava.

At the moment, I'd give anything for those.

Honestly, though, I know deep down that Ava's attitude is mostly coming from a place of hurt, of mistrust. (Some of it is likely the result of being a preteen girl, which I can't do anything about!)

So instead of being perturbed by her like she probably wants, I sit down on her black comforter, against her oak headboard. "Okay." Propping up my feet, I place my hands behind my head as I snuggle into the pillows at my back. "Guess I will too."

She turns and stares at me. "What are you doing?"

"I thought we were staying here."

"*I'm* staying here."

"Well, my job right now is to be where you are. So if you're here, then so am I." There's nothing a preteen hates more than uninvited company, right? I sure hope so in Ava's case.

And just to pretend like I have no stakes in the game, I let my gaze wander all around her room. But calling it "her room" is definitely the wrong descriptor, because with the dark accent table and dresser, the blank white walls, and the bookcase filled with medical textbooks, it's obvious that this is just a guest room turned emergency bedroom.

Hmmm. "Hey, what would you do with this room if you had a choice?"

"What do you mean?" She says it like I've just insulted her, quick and gruff.

I shrug and wave my finger around. "Like, what colors would you pick? You know, to decorate with." I tap my chin. "If I had a room of my own—"

"You don't?"

"Not at the moment. I'm living with my sister. She really loves bright colors. Like, her furniture is hot pink."

Ava's nose scrunches. "Really?"

"I know, not my cup of tea either. I mean, bright colors have their place, but I like softer shades for my bedroom. Things that are calming, you know? When I'm in my room, I want to feel safe, like it's my retreat, a place to let down my hair and just be."

Her pointer finger runs up and down the smooth surface of her earbud as her gaze sweeps the room. "That makes sense." Then, as if realizing that she's having an actual conversation with me, she stands. "Not like it matters anyway. I don't get the things I want. And this isn't my room. It's Uncle Ryan's."

Then she walks out.

Well, at least I got her up and out of her room. I'll take my wins where I can get them.

Within fifteen minutes, we've piled into my car and are on the way to the social worker's office, which is in between the house and the hospital where Ryan works as an ER doctor. (He and I didn't actually get into very much detail about his life last night. He was clearly exhausted and I figured he could fill me in on everything later if he wanted to. I just know he's an ER doctor because Lauren bumped her head once and he was the one who treated her.)

I glance in the rearview mirror. Ava's earbuds are in again and she's staring out the window. No expression. Just a mask on the outside. What's going on in that head of hers?

Mila, on the other hand, tells me every single last thought, so I don't have to wonder. By the time we pull into the office complex's sparsely populated parking lot, she's told me what she wants to be when she grows up (a unicorn trainer), where she wants to live (at the end of a rainbow, naturally), what her favorite movie is (going old school with *The Little Mermaid*), and all about the ladybug she saw and followed around at recess yesterday.

The girl is a talkative Energizer Bunny on steroids.

I turn off the ignition. "All right, ladies, let's find your uncle."

We start to climb from the vehicle when Ryan's black

Ford pickup pulls up next to us. Can I just say? There's something about a man with a pickup. Brooks was all into his shiny Corvette, but an F-150 is a thrilling thing of power. Especially when it comes with a good old country boy whose perfect manners match his perfect muscles.

Never thought I'd be that girl, but here I am.

He turns off the engine and hops out, whisking around toward us wearing the scrubs and zip-up gray hoodie he left in this morning. "Hey, y'all."

Y'all. I can't even. "Hey," I squeak out, then clear my throat. "How was work?"

"Fine." Grimacing, he waves a hand as if work isn't worth a mention, and I wonder if there's a story there. And if so, will I ever get to hear it? Or will I just be the girl who helped him out for a few days one time in January? The thought leaves an unfathomable pit in my stomach. No, I'm not going to let him—at the very least, these girls—be strangers after this.

Great. It's been less than twenty-four hours and already I'm smitten with them all.

Mila runs to Ryan and hugs him around the middle, and Ava slinks toward the front doors of the tall office building like a prisoner walking toward her execution. As he hugs his youngest niece back, Ryan meets my gaze. "How was this little lady?"

"Obviously, she's just a complete terror. I don't know how you stand being around her."

Looking up at me, Mila laughs. "Miss Kenny!"

"I know what you mean." Ryan tosses his niece up onto his shoulders. "She's a real monster."

Mila's giggling hysterically now. "I am not! I'm a unicorn!"

We start walking toward the building. "I thought you were going to *train* unicorns," I say, tapping my chin.

"I am."

"So you *are* a unicorn, *and* you're going to train them?"

"Duh, silly. Everybody knows that trainers hafta know what unicorns like if they wanna do a good job. And how else am I gonna know what a unicorn likes unless I *am* one?"

His arms braced over Mila's knees, Ryan glances at me, a serious look on his face. "I mean, she has a fair point."

I nod. "She really does."

We all laugh and he puts Mila down once we get inside the cold building. She runs toward the elevator where Ava waits.

He snags my elbow to stop me from going any further. The contact, small as it might be, steals my breath. What is with my crazy reaction to this man? Maybe it's just that he's the first guy to show me any attention after Brooks broke my heart. "So ... did it really go okay? How was Ava?"

"It went great. Mila's full of energy, and Ava is ... well, a preteen. But I think I'm getting through to her."

"I'm not surprised. You're so ..."

"So ...?" I cross my arms and tilt my head, holding back a smile. (I kind of want to smile a lot when I'm around him.) "Should I be offended by what you were just going to say?"

"No! Not at all." He sticks his hands into his hoodie pockets. "I was going to say perceptive. You seem to have a knack for knowing what people need."

"Oh. Um, thank you." I can feel my cheeks warm, though I'm not sure why. My sister has told me the same thing. I bite my lip and push my hair behind my ear. "Well, I'd better let you get to the meeting with the social worker."

"Right! Yeah." He clears his throat. "Thanks again for today. I can't tell you what a relief it was. My boss was not going to be happy if I had to take off more time, though he says he understands …"

I place my hand on his upper arm and *oh my biceps*. How often does this guy have to work out to get arms like this? *Focus, Kennedy!* "I meant it last night when I said I was happy to help. And I'm happy to help tomorrow too."

"Even after today? Are you sure?"

"Absolutely."

"Would you …" He looks away, down the hall where the girls are standing. The elevator doors still haven't opened, which seems a bit ridiculous considering there are only a few people here (if the half-empty parking lot is any indication). Then his attention comes back to me, and mine to him. "Would you want to stay for dinner tomorrow after I get home?"

Did he just ask me on a date? Before I can open my mouth to exclaim a resounding "Yes!", he rushes on.

"For all of us, I mean. All four of us. The girls can eat, um, also. If that's okay."

Oh. So not a date.

Although, with the way he's looking at me—soft around the eyes, which are shining with something like hope—maybe he just thinks I'd say no if he asked me on a proper date.

Yeah, hi. Has the guy looked in the mirror lately? "I'd love to stay for dinner."

"Great. What's your favorite place to eat? I'll get takeout."

"Oh, it doesn't matter. Whatever the girls like."

He studies me for a moment, then shakes his head. "No, this is to say thank you for all you've done. So you get to pick."

That … is the sweetest. And something I'm not used to. Let's just say Brooks had his opinions, and it was easier to just go with them. "I'll have to think about it."

He points at me. "I'll be watching for a text." Then he slips on one of those little half smiles and starts walking backward toward the girls, but facing me. "Goodnight, Miss Kenny."

I laugh. "Goodnight, Dr. Ryan."

"I heard a little rumor." Princess Chloe Huntington flops down stomach first onto my bed in her monogrammed hot pink pajamas—yes, even her pajamas are fashionable. Her long blonde curls hang over her silky shoulders and fall onto Alexis's bright green comforter as Chloe props her chin up with her hand. Those blue eyes of hers sparkle with mischief. "And it has to do with you and that brilliantly sexy doctor next door." Her British-like accent lilts across the room.

I keep folding my basket of laundry from my spot on the other half of the bed. "I don't know what you're talking about."

One perfectly plucked eyebrow lifts. "Don't try denying it. Tia saw you over there earlier today."

Directing my attention to the doorway, I catch sight of Chloe's bodyguard standing just outside in the hallway. Despite the shadows, her dark skin and prominent cheekbones stand out against the stark white wall, and the dark jeans and blazer she wears don't help either. But let's just say I wouldn't want to meet that woman in an alley—dark or well-lit. If I were a threat to the royal family, that is.

I lean in and lower my voice. "Does she really have to follow you around the house?"

"Don't change the subject, Kennedy." Chloe's eyes flit to the doorway and back again. "But let's just say she takes her job extremely seriously. It's not as if I have any desire to run off. I'm mostly here to keep Lauren calm for the next few months until the wedding. It just gets ghastly boring during the day when you're all working. I've already shopped my way across the city."

I fluff out a pair of jeans and fold them in half, then half again. "I thought you had all of your charity work back home to keep you busy."

"I do, but sometimes I wish ..." A strained smile crosses her face, wrinkling her smooth brow for a moment. I've never asked her exact age, but I don't think she's a day over thirty. Still, the burdens she must carry ... well, I'm glad I'm not royalty. If she's seeking a reprieve from royal life, then I'm glad she's found it here—even if she *does* have to travel with a bodyguard.

Guess I should give her the distraction she needs. "And yes, I was over at Ryan's house today helping to watch his nieces. He's got temporary custody while his sister is working through a few things." Even though I know Chloe wouldn't tell a soul, Ryan didn't give me permission to share the details of his sister's struggles with anyone else. And there's something that makes me protective of what others might think of his family if they knew his sister was in jail.

"Nieces?" Chloe whistles. "I assumed they were his girlfriend's children. So he's single, then?"

"I don't know about that, but the woman we've seen coming and going is his sister, Sophie. And the girls are Ava and Mila." I set the jeans onto a pile of other folded pants and move on to some of my unmentionables. Alexis teases me for my skimpy underwear—she prefers what I call the grandma variety—but even if nobody ever sees me wearing it again, I like that it makes me feel secretly powerful. "They're the sweetest girls."

"Even the grouchy-looking older one?"

"Well." I grit my teeth, widen my eyes, and suck in an exaggerated groan. "No, I'm kidding. I think she's just hurting, to be honest."

"And a preteen girl. Blimey, I don't wish those hormones on my worst enemy."

"So much truth in that statement." Chuckling, I stand and grab the small stack of underwear, heading for the dresser in the corner. When I moved in a few months ago, Alexis graciously allotted me half of her space—the other two bedrooms in her house are currently being shared by Shelby and Lauren, and Tia and Chloe, so her room is the only place for me.

"Sooooo." Chloe rolls over, sits up against the pillows, and twirls a lock of her hair. "Does this mean you'll be working for the good doctor indefinitely?"

The top dresser drawer sticks as I close it. "What?" I toss a hip and it ekes shut. "Oh, I'm not working for him. His nanny quit at the last minute and I'm just helping out for a few days until he finds someone new."

"But weren't you considering getting a second job?" She pulls her knees into her chest. "Or have you decided to take up dear old granny on her offer?"

I snort and round the bed for another pile of clothing that needs to be put away. "You know that's not happening. At least not right now. I'm not ready to leave San Diego yet." Gran's offer of a job at Montgomery Inc. in San Francisco would be sweet if it wasn't motivated by her desire to control me—the way she was never able to control Mom.

Even if it would mean only working for a few years before I could afford to pay for college in its entirety.

"Because of Dr. Ryan?" Chloe teases.

Picking up my pile of jeans—most of them from hot boutiques in the Bay area who wanted a social media shoutout—I roll my eyes. "Because my sister is here." The jeans take up a little more than half the space in the bottom drawer, encroaching on Alexis's territory. I frown. She probably would never say it, but I know sometimes she misses having her own place to retreat to. Squatting, I attempt to maneuver the pile over a bit so it leaves more space for Alexis's things. Then I stand and brush off my hands. "Besides, this town is where Mom and I finally settled down in the few years before she died."

"Not to mention you'd have to work with your smarmy ex if you moved back."

Oh yeah. There's that too. Brooks is an attorney at Montgomery Inc. Sometimes I wonder if that's why he dated me in the first place—to land a cushy in-house counsel job at one of the best companies in San Francisco. "I really have no desire to be in the same city as him again, much less work in the same building day in and day out."

"I don't blame you. He sounds like a real blighter."

"He is." Joining her on the bed, I prop my head against the headboard. "And yet, I was with him for nearly two years. What does that say about me?"

She lays her head on my shoulder, and the scent of her mandarin orange lotion teases my nose. "It says that you're much too forgiving and sweet. Loyal, perhaps a bit to a fault?"

"Alexis may have said something similar before. She hated Brooks, but tried to like him for my sake. Same with my mom. I don't think Alexis was crazy about her either."

"From what you've told me, she was fun at least."

"Yeah. She was that." Fun and dynamic and spontaneous—and needy, too. Dependent on man after man, seeking "the one" who would finally make her happy enough to stay. By the time I was eighteen, we'd lived with at least six different men—powerful ones who worked for Hollywood, CEOs of big pharma companies, all people who could provide her with the lifestyle she was "used to"—and she'd seriously dated dozens more.

And yet, despite her faults, I still miss her like crazy. Or maybe I just miss the feeling of belonging to somebody who never viewed me as a burden. Of having a home. Though to be honest, none of the places I've ever lived has felt like a real home. Even this, here, is Alexis's home. Not mine.

Of course I'm grateful to her. And love her. But sometimes, I just feel so … smothered.

My breath struggles in and out for a moment, but Chloe's touch on my hand grounds me. Once I have hold of my emotions, I squeeze and straighten. "Anyway, back to your original question—yeah, I need to find another job in addition to Java Awakening. I'm barely able to pay my bills, and I have a long way to go until I can afford even a year of school."

"I still can't believe your grandmother won't release your trust fund. Isn't there some sort of age clause? Many of my friends received their inheritances when they turned twenty-one."

"Have you forgotten my grandmother relishes control? She designed the trust, which means she can basically hold onto it until I meet her requirements."

"And just what are those again?"

"It's all very vague. Basically, I have to 'prove myself respectable,'" I say in a haughty tone with my nose tilted to the ceiling fan. "And let's just say that the great Marsha Montgomery does not find coffee-making and the service industry respectable for 'someone of my bloodline.'"

But unless I'm willing to go work for her, I have no other way to pay for college—the one thing that might actually earn her respect. Of course, I could always apply for loans but with my history, I don't think I'd qualify. Who would take a chance on someone who's already partied herself out of enrollment once?

And what if I can't hack it again? What if … I fail?

It's one reason I won't let Alexis pay for my schooling, even though she's offered multiple times. If I fail using my own money, at least the only one up a creek is … me.

"Ah, all this talk of bloodlines is making me feel right at home." Chloe scoffs. "Believe me, I know all about family duty." She gets a far-off look in her eye for a moment. "At least yours won't stop you from being with the man you've fancied forever."

Hmm. I can't help but wonder if the spark I saw between Chloe and Frederick (her brother Topher's best friend and bodyguard) back at Thanksgiving might have been real. If so … poor friend. I don't know all of her country's rules about royalty, but there must be a thousand reasons why the two of them can't be together.

From the hallway, Tia grunts.

Chloe shakes the reverie from her eyes and looks at me again, forcing a smile. "Which means you're free to go after Dr. Ryan. Or at the very least, get him to employ you."

"Employ me?"

"You said he was seeking a nanny, yeah?"

"Well … yes." My mouth is suddenly very dry and I turn to my side table for my insulated cup, taking a sip. It does nothing to help. "But I'm hardly qualified."

"Why not? You're brilliant, and a fine role model for those girls."

"Okay, what are you smoking, Princess Chloe? Or maybe you've got a fever?" I lift my hand to her forehead.

She pushes my hand away. "I mean it, Ken. Look at you. You are a sincere, wonderful person who's yeah, maybe had some bad judgment when it comes to love. But who among us hasn't? So ask Ryan if you can be the girls' new nanny. What's more respectable than working for a doctor?"

She has a point. While being a nanny isn't like having a corporate job, Gran *does* have a certain reverence for physicians. Maybe having one for a boss would score me points. At the very least, it might get her off my back. Stop the passive-aggressive text messages.

But … "It's only temporary. The girls are here for just six months."

"Well, that's a decent chunk of time to save some money, yeah? And to figure out what Kennedy wants. Because that does matter, you know. You don't have to do what everyone else wants to do, or wants *you* to do."

She sighs. "*You* have a choice." And I can hear what she's not saying—*unlike me*.

What Kennedy wants ... Hmmm. I honestly haven't thought about that in a long while—not from a healthy place, anyway. A place that wasn't actively grieving, which is something I've been doing for so many years, it seems.

Now, I'm free to choose.

And that's almost more terrifying than hands that are tied.

four

· · ·

ALL DAY, I've been thinking about what Chloe said last night—that I should do what I want.

That I should ask Ryan to hire me.

It seems kind of bold, doesn't it? But my social media feed is filled with people telling me to go after what I want. Still, I didn't know what that was for sure until today.

After spending the morning serving at the coffee shop, I picked up Mila from school (turns out, her school is attached to Ava's K-8 school—which also happens to be the same place where both Shelby and Eric are teachers!) and we made a stop at the store for a frozen pizza and all the junk food we could carry. We got home right about twenty minutes before Ava was walking up from the bus stop, which meant I was able to keep her from scampering off to her room.

Then we sat and ate pizza (it was only slightly crispy

around the edges because I might have forgotten to set the oven timer—oops). Mila did my hair, and I gave both of them makeovers while a movie played in the background. I honestly couldn't even tell you which one, because we didn't pay much attention to it. Just talked about our days, including my commentary on the funniest coffee shop patrons I encountered and Mila's demonstration of the "Wiggle Song" she learned at school. Even Ava joined the conversation, supplying a very enthusiastic "School was boring" to our chatter. (Okay, I'm clearly being sarcastic about her enthusiasm, but she *did* stay in the same room and once or twice I caught the hint of a smile cross her lips. I'm calling it a win.)

So, yeah. Now it's hours later, and I'm sitting here on the couch with my arms around a napping Mila—who's adorned in glittery eye shadow and bright red lips—and I'm helping Ava with her math homework whenever she has a question. And it hits me square in the chest: I *want* to be a freaking nanny.

A nanny.

But not a nanny to just anyone. Specifically, a nanny to these girls—to Ava and Mila—who need someone to be here for them.

Why *not* me? After all, I might not know what it is to have an addict for a mom, but I know what it's like to lose people you love in one way or another. Know what it's like to feel abandoned. To have to grow up way too quickly.

It's kind of ridiculous when you think about it, but

despite the fact it's only been two days, these two have already burrowed their way into my heart—them and their adorably sexy uncle.

Not that he can be part of the equation.

Because if he ends up being my boss, then he can't also be my boyfriend. He can't be someone I flirt with. He can't even be someone I fantasize about. I don't want a guy to have the power to affect my career ever again like Brooks did—even if the career is only meant to be temporary.

Besides, falling for your boss just gets ... complicated. I saw that the few times my mom got involved with hers over the years. It never ended well. Not that Ryan has indicated he's interested in dating me, but it would be dumb of me to even entertain the idea. I've let one too many men throw my life off track. It's not happening again, thank you very much.

I yawn and stretch my neck from side to side. Finley is lying on my feet, keeping my bare toes warm. The waning light of day meanders through the windows, a reminder that the cares of the week have drifted away, and the weekend has finally arrived. Ava has in her beloved earbuds, so other than Mila's sweet breathing and a low buzzing coming from the TV, everything is quiet—until the front door opens in the foyer.

Immediately, Finley leaps up to investigate. Shoes squeak on the tile and Ryan appears in the archway carrying two large plastic bags of food from my favorite local taco place. I release Mila's curls to wave a hand at him.

Setting the bags on the counter, he walks over, taking in the sight on the now visible side of the couch. "Hey," he whispers.

"Hey."

And there's an unbroken moment suspended there between us, where we're both speaking without words. It's a language I don't yet understand. Maybe with time …

"Hey, Uncle Ryan."

We both blink and move our gazes toward Ava, who pops out her earbuds and closes her math text. "Thank goodness. I'm starving."

I laugh. "We just ate some pizza not that long ago."

She wrinkles her nose. "It was burnt."

"Ava, don't be rude," Ryan gently scolds.

"It's okay." I wink at her. "It was."

"Well, these tacos sure aren't. They smell delicious. I had to stop myself from sampling them on the drive home."

"Mmm. I haven't had them in a few weeks." I draw my finger down Mila's nose, mimicking the way my mom used to rouse me when I was little and had fallen asleep somewhere. She starts to move.

"I've never had them."

"I'm sorry, what?" My fingers still and I glance at where he stands at the counter, unpacking the bags. The plastic rustles beneath his fingertips. "And you've lived here *how* long?"

"Since college." He holds up a brown paper sack with grease spots at the bottom. "Here, Ava. Try one."

Reaching in, he grabs a chip and crunches into it, then groans. "Oh, wow."

"Told you. They make their own tortillas and chips fresh every day."

Mila's trying to turn into the couch cushions and I scoop her up and stand. She slumps against me, and I whisper into her hair. "Mila, love, it's time to eat. Again."

Immediately, her eyes pop open and she sits up, grabbing me around the neck. "I want more gummy worms, Miss Kenny."

"Shhh." I see Ryan's watching us with an amused expression. "You weren't supposed to tell your uncle about that."

While Ava digs into the bag of chips like she's a teen boy on a fast—apparently preteen girls can pack it away too—Ryan approaches sleepy Mila and me. "Hey, sweetie. Did you have a good day?" When he leans in and strokes her hair, he also sets one hand against my lower back.

I'm not sure if he realizes it, but I definitely do. My whole body lights up like it's the Titanic on her maiden voyage.

Of course, we all know how *that* turned out.

Future boss—hopefully. Remember? I scold my subconscious. *Now step away from the handsome doctor.* But that vixen inside of me has a mind of her own, and we stay right there until Ryan lifts Mila from my arms and heads back toward the food. He sets her gently in her chair at the four-person table that fits perfectly in the kitchen alcove surrounded by windows.

While I pull Styrofoam containers from the plastic bags, he dishes up drinks from the fridge and soon we're all sitting with full plates at the table. The girls tell us about their days, and even though I've heard a lot of it already (at least from Mila … Ava is still pretty quiet), I don't mind one bit.

When Mila switches to talking about what we did together, I find Ryan's eyes on me—and the attention is too much. I give my *al pastor* tacos all my love, which isn't *that* hard to do, considering they're bursting with the flavor of sliced onion, pineapple, and cilantro.

"What about you?" I ask during a lull in the conversation—aka, when Mila finally takes a bite of her food and realizes she's hungry. "How was work?"

And there once again is a down turn of his lips, only for a second before he plunges on with a laugh and a silly story about a little boy who got a bean stuck up his nose. But my thoughts can't help but linger there, on the frown. Maybe he doesn't like his job?

Before I know it, this thoroughly delightful evening meal is over. I almost wish we'd eaten on real dishes so the cleanup would take longer, but by the time Ryan gets Mila down for bed and Ava has headed toward her room for the night, the kitchen is sparkling and I've been sitting on the couch ignoring a text from Gran—*"Just say yes, Kennedy. You know you want to."*—and resisting the urge to mindlessly scroll social media for quite some time.

When Ryan finally walks back into the room, looking deliciously casual in sweatpants and a white T-shirt, he jumps at the sight of me. "Oh, hey. I didn't know you were still here."

I laugh and set my phone down. "Did you think I was the kind of girl who just left without saying goodbye?"

Something ticks in his jaw and I wonder what nerve I've unexpectedly hit. "No, of course not. I just …" He tilts his head, then motions toward the back door. "Do you have a little time to talk?"

"Of course." I bite my lip. "I just need to run to my car to grab a jacket really quick."

"Here." He snatches an extra sweatshirt—the red Oklahoma University one he wore when I first met him —off the large chair and holds it out for me. "I'm sure it'll be huge on you, but it's super warm."

Um, yes, please. "Okay. Thanks." I slip it over my head and he's right—it absolutely swallows me, going to mid-thigh, with the sleeves completely covering my hands. But it smells divine, like wood sage and sea salt. *I'm sorry, Dr. Ryan, but you're never getting this sweatshirt back again,* the vixen coos.

"I'm not, huh?"

Ooo. "I said that out loud, didn't I?"

He opens the back door and a breeze lifts his curls. Then he winks. "Don't worry." Ryan leans toward me and tugs on one of the strings near the hood. "I thought it was cute."

Normally, a woman hates to be called cute. Sexy? Yep. Enticing? You bet. But cute is the equivalent of a pat on the head and a shove out the door.

Not when Dr. Ryan Rosche says it, though. When he

says it, with that dreamy drawl, his warm blue eyes on me, it makes me want an engraved plaque to hang on my wall that says, "Kennedy Matkin: World's Cutest Woman."

My eyes widen and I quickly move through the doorway out into the brisk air. Good. Cold air is good, because I was just about to blurt out a very un-thought-through statement. Something completely inane like, "Will you marry me?" or "Sure, I'll have your babies."

Lowering myself onto a porch swing that is a bit rusted but still looks solid enough, I fold my arms across my chest and snuggle into the sweatshirt that is now mine forever. Ryan sits beside me—not super close, but not as far as I'd have thought he would if he wanted to keep things distinctly friend-like between us.

Finley follows us out and curls up just outside the door like the sweet doggy protector he is. A clear sky greets us overhead, and crickets chirp in the yard.

"So." I plant a foot on the concrete slab and rock the swing back and forth ever so slightly. "What did you want to talk about?"

The lights are on in Alexis's house, and I can hear female laughter drifting from the windows.

It takes him a while to answer. "They just seem really happy. The girls, I mean. You're so good with them."

"So are you. You're a wonderful uncle."

"I want to be. I obviously don't have kids of my own, and those girls are my world." He sighs and joins me in foot rocking the swing. "I hate what Sophie's actions have done to them, but she's hurting too, you know? I just wish I knew how to protect them from all of it." His right hand fists the part of his pants covering his thigh.

"You're doing great. No one can protect someone else from everything. All you can do is provide a safe place for them to come home to every day." I lean closer and place my hand over his. "And you have."

Ryan glances down at my hand. Maybe I shouldn't have touched him—maybe I made it weird. But when I try to pull away, he grabs my fingers and holds my palm against his.

My breath catches.

His seems to as well, until he clears his throat and looks away, up at the constellations in their homes. Unlike me, they know exactly where they belong. And aside from the fact that Ryan's gaze is fixed there, I'm suddenly jealous of the stars.

Hey, I never said I was normal.

"Kennedy, this is going to sound really strange."

"But …?"

With his free hand, he rubs his slightly stubbled chin. Sitting as close as I am, even in the moonlight, I see the tiny blond hairs. Are they as rough as they look? My fingers itch to find out. "I don't usually say this much, but you're easy to talk to. I mean, I kinda feel like I've known you my whole life."

Oh my sheesh. I open my mouth to respond. Close it again. What's a girl to say to something like that? But if I don't say *something,* then another inane comment is bound to come out—something like "Yes, you absolutely may kiss me, please and thank you." Which would not exactly help me get that nanny gig. He'd think I'm not mentally stable enough to watch his nieces.

So, naturally, I release his hand and respond with a joke. "Well, not your *whole* life."

His nose scrunches and he pivots sideways in his seat to better take me in. "What do you mean?"

"Just that it would be hard to have known me your whole life, considering I'm a lot younger than you."

He chuckles. "A few years is hardly a lot younger."

A few years? I'm slightly amused by how egregiously off base his assumptions are. Unless I'm wrong and he's not as old as I think. "You're what? Thirty-three?"

"Thirty-four."

Nailed it. "And just how old do you think I am, Dr. Ryan?"

His eyes seem to spark at my teasing. "I'm really bad at guessing ages, and I know you aren't supposed to ask a woman how old she is. My mom did manage to teach me a thing or two before she died."

"Wait. Your mom died?" I can't help myself. It just pops out. But now that he mentions it, he did say something about his parents being gone, didn't he? I just assumed he meant they lived far away. "Your dad too?"

"Yeah. When I was eleven." His throat bobs. "Car accident."

So young. "My dad died when I was four in a plane crash. My mom when I was eighteen."

A breeze kisses my cheeks, and laughter from Alexis's house breaks through the silence of the moment—a silence that isn't awkward in the least. It's the silence of two people who are both orphans, who understand one another, though their circumstances were likely very different. (For example, I'm guessing by the way he talks that his parents were actually married and still in love.)

And yet. There's comfort in knowing you aren't the only one.

"I'm sorry," he says.

"I'm sorry too."

And that's it. No unnecessary platitudes about seeing them again one day or being thankful for the days we did have. Just open honesty—*I can't fix it, but I'm sorry.*

"You know," he continues, "I think losing my parents so young is one reason I have to make things different for Ava and Mila. I don't want them growing up with the same burdens I did. That Sophie did. Our parents' death ruined her." Once more, his hand brushes that stubble and I have to sit on my own to keep from reaching for him. "Their dad already walked out on them. I don't want this to be the thing that breaks their spirits."

"It won't. Because you're here and you love them. That's enough."

His harsh laugh cuts the night air in half and he stops the gentle swaying of the swing as he plants his foot hard on the ground. "Theoretically, maybe. But what kind of guardian am I if I can't even find a consistent nanny?"

If ever there was the perfect segue to what I was

hoping to discuss, this is it. "You haven't found a replacement yet?"

He shakes his head. "It's not easy to find someone who's willing to work such a weird schedule."

Hold up. "Weird?"

"I guess more like inconsistent. I sometimes have overnight shifts, even a few 24-hour shifts thrown in there. If we're backed up, I get off late, and sometimes I get called in at the last minute or have to leave super early before the girls are up. It changes all the time."

Yikes. I got so used to being my own boss as an influencer that even adjusting to working at the coffee shop was a bit rough at first. Of course, the structure has been a blessing, especially since Josh keeps my hours mostly the same—or he will, now that he's back from paternity leave. But Ryan's schedule sounds like a nightmare, especially if he doesn't care for his job, like I suspect. "That sounds rough for *you*."

"I've gotten used to it." But has he? "I have a spare room here for a nanny to sleep in. She could even move in if I felt like it would be a good situation for the girls. But it's just difficult to find someone willing and able to do that who I also feel comfortable with, you know? The last nanny only worked a few days. Not even enough time to consider moving in."

I freeze. A spare room … my *own* room. Alexis could have her space back. I wouldn't have to pay rent anymore—not that she makes me anyway, but I insist. This is all working out better than I could have dreamed.

Now I just have to convince Ryan that this is the

right move, even if it means ignoring whatever chemistry I think I'm feeling between us. "Maybe you'll think this is a terrible idea, but I have actually been looking— well, not actively looking, I guess, but thinking about looking—for another job. Mine is great and all, but I don't get enough hours to fill my time. Or my bank account. I need something else to supplement my income, so I can save for college."

He just blinks at me. Waits.

"I mean, my rich grandma back in San Francisco offered me a job, but my ex works at the company and I'd rather not deal with him. And I kind of like it in San Diego, and I don't know, today I just really enjoyed my time with the girls." I hesitate. Here goes nothing. "Do you think—"

"Are you serious?" He braces his arm against the back of the swing, leans in. "Would you really consider helping me with them on a longer-term basis? I've wanted to ask you all night, but didn't want to take advantage of your kind nature."

I smile at his description of me. It's just so … sweet. "I think this is a situation that could benefit us both."

"But it's just for six months. After that, Sophie will be released and you'll be out of a job."

"I know."

"I'd pay you this time. It'd be a legit job." He names an amount that's far more generous than I was expecting.

Now I'm the one bracing myself. I grip the slats of wood underneath me. "That seems like too much."

"It's what I was paying the other nanny. I'm asking

you to be available at all hours, so it seems more than fair to me."

I do some quick calculations in my head and mentally squeal. If I'm not paying rent to Alexis anymore, and I keep working at Java Awakening the days that Mila is in school, I could have enough money saved to attend college in the fall. "If you're sure," I say in my most mature voice. It still trembles a bit, but I can't keep my feelings bottled up.

If she's there, I'm going to hug Chloe when I get back tonight. Girlfriend is brilliant.

"Okay. I accept."

"Great. That's … thank you, Kennedy. Should we agree on a probation period first? Say, a month? That way, if anything changes on your part—"

"—or you want to get rid of me?" I tease.

"Well, that's unlikely. But a probation period gives the girls and us a chance to try this out long-term. I don't want you to feel stuck here if another job opportunity comes up that you like better."

"It won't, but I'm okay with a probation period. A month works for me." I cock my head. "When do you want me to move in?"

"Oh."

I squint. "Oh, what?"

"I guess I thought with you living right next door that you wouldn't need to move in."

Huh. I guess that could work. But then I hear Chloe's voice in my head, encouraging me to ask for what I want, and I inhale a breath before plowing on. "Actually, I'd love to move out of my sister's room. She's been awesome to have me, but me being there was never supposed to be permanent. You said yourself that you want someone you feel comfortable with, who could be there at all hours, right?"

"Well, yes, but—"

"But what? Is there a reason you don't want me there?" Oh goodness, what if there is? Here I've been thinking we were completely at ease with each other, that I fit pretty well into their lives, but maybe it's all in my head. How embarrassing would that be?

But no, he said he felt like he'd known me forever. That has to be a good thing, right?

Ryan waits an inordinately long amount of time. I wish I could dig around in his brain, hear what he's thinking. But he just swallows and whispers, "Not if things stay … professional between us."

Gah. It's like he's just shown me his cards—and after dating Brooks, I didn't think men did that. Even after living together for over a year, I still didn't understand that man as well as I understand Ryan right now.

He likes me too. And he's afraid of crossing some line if I move in.

But here's the thing. I may like him, sure. But I *do* need this to stay professional whether I move in or not, because he's going to be my boss. Thankfully, I've already decided that. And I'm resolved to do it. I just have to keep my distance from this man for the next six months. How hard can that be?

So I nod. Hold out my hand. "Professional works for me."

I'm sure I'm imagining the disappointment in his

eyes, but then he takes my hand in his and we shake. "You've got yourself a deal."

The way he says it—all low and throaty and sexy Southern—makes me almost regret what I say next. "And you've got yourself a nanny."

five

. . .

"THIS MIGHT JUST BE the dumbest idea you've ever had, Kennedy."

Well, I knew this conversation was bound to happen once I told my sister about the new job. I shake my head and turn from her, straining to reach the extra box of clothes I stored on an upper shelf in her garage. "Tell me how you really feel, Alexis."

"We're sisters." Alexis, her hair a deep orange color this week (it changes regularly), grabs a short ladder that's leaning against the far wall and brings it to me. "We tell each other the truth, even if the other doesn't like it."

The brilliant blue sky shimmers through the open garage door, an encouragement to leave the cold dankness of the corner where I'm trying to gather the rest of my stuff for packing. Since Ryan doesn't work this weekend, I'm taking the day to move my things over. Then I'll likely spend one more night here with Alexis.

I'm totally sure this is the right move.

But apparently my sister thinks I'm making a mistake. What else is new?

"Like how I told you Dax might be good for you?" I unfurl the ladder just beneath the box I'm aiming for. "And that you needed to forgive Dad to move on with your life? And how I—"

"Yeah, yeah. Exactly." Without me asking her to, Alexis steadies the ladder so I can climb up it. That's one thing I love about her—she anticipates the needs of those around her. And she'd do anything for us. Even tie us up and keep us in a room alone if she thought it was the best thing for us.

Let's just call her a strong personality, though Dax has softened her a bit, I must admit.

"And now *I'm* telling you that moving in with a man you just met is an epically stupid thing to do."

And yeah—believe it or not, *that's* softened.

I grunt as I tug on the huge cardboard box labeled Spring Clothes. Did I put bricks in this thing? "I didn't *just* meet him."

"Uh, basically. I've lived next door to him for years and we've never spoken. What does that say about him?"

I glance down into my sister's brown eyes that match my own. We don't look that much alike, each mostly taking after our moms, but the eyes—those are all Matkin. And I know that she's saying what others might believe are mean things, but I see the worry behind it. It's there, lurking in the narrowed corners.

Unfortunately, that worry is present a lot when I'm

around. Being nine years older, she thinks it's her job to take care of me. And yes, I've not made it easy to be my sister. I've been stupid in the past. Reckless. But doesn't she see I'm changing? That I'm trying to be responsible?

Frowning, I give all my attention to the box, the back end of which appears to be stuck on some sort of divot in the shelving unit. "I think it says more about you, actually. You have to admit, until recently—until Dax— you weren't overly fond of the male species." I pull. Still stuck. "And you kind of, shall we say, treated them all like garbage? I don't blame Ryan for not talking to you. He was probably scared you'd bite his head off."

I give one last tug, and the box comes free. But the momentum leaves me wobbling on the ladder until Alexis rounds it quickly and presses her hand firmly against my lower back. Rescuing me. Again.

"Then he's not man enough for you to live with," she says in a low voice.

I huff and hand her the box. "Come on, A. I'm not living with him. Not like that." Not like Brooks. "I'm taking a job that has certain requirements, and that's one of them."

"He'd better not be requiring certain *other* things or I'll—"

"Come on!" I descend the ladder and plant my hands on my hips. "What kind of girl do you think I am?"

She drops my box onto the concrete floor of the garage and crosses her arms. "The kind easily swayed by handsome men."

Doesn't she see that that's ice to my heart? That she's

basically saying I'm just like my mother? I shoot her a glare.

"Don't look at me like that. Stooks"—our nickname for Stupid Brooks—"had you under some kind of spell." The last word wobbles from her mouth and she presses her lips together.

And all the fire goes out of me. In the heat of moments like this, when I'm trying so hard to defend my decisions to the one person I respect and love more than anyone else in this world, it's easy to forget that we are on the same team. That everything she does and says is because she loves me just as fiercely as I love her. That despite all that's happened to us—all that our parents have put us through—we've chosen each other.

I step forward and grab her into a hug. "This is different, okay?"

It takes her a minute but her arms come up and around me too. I can feel her breathing steady.

And I continue. "Ryan and I aren't in a relationship. He's my boss. I'm just moving over there to take care of those girls. So I can save money for college."

"You don't have to sell your soul to do that. I said I'd pay for it."

"Alexis," I groan. "I'm an adult woman. I can pay my own way. And I'm not selling my soul." She's so dramatic. I pull back and smile. "But look! You're getting your room back. This should make you happy. Your little sister is moving on with life. Taking care of herself. And I'm doing it all from the comfort of the house right next door, where you can still spy on me and pretend you aren't."

She sniffs, something she never used to do. Proof of the softening. "I don't do that."

"Aw, you're cute when you lie."

"Just promise me you'll be careful."

"I will." I bop her nose like she used to do to me when I was little, then turn and pick up my box. Huh. No bricks after all. Just lots of clothing. And I know I could keep it here in this garage, but I want that room in Ryan's house to feel like mine, like some sort of retreat of my own. So I don't want to leave any pieces of my life behind, even if it's only next door. "He really is a good guy. I'll be safe."

"But will your heart? I know you, Kennedy. You give your entire self to people."

If she'd seen me getting cozy next to him on the swing last night, she'd definitely be readying some rope. "Of course I do." I wink in an over-exaggerated manner. "That's what someone else taught me to do."

"You were already like that when we met at dad's funeral."

"I was four." I think of Mila and my insides turn to goo. "Four-year-olds have never met a stranger. It's when we get older that we change. And you helped me to stay grounded."

"You did the same for me." She presses a hand beneath her eyes, where a few tears have fallen. Then she shakes her head and moves to take the box from me.

I maneuver out of the way. "I've got this. How about I get things moved over to Ryan's and then we order a pizza and watch a movie tonight together? I'll even let you pick one of your terrible thriller movies."

Before she can respond, a car pulls into her driveway.

I know who that car belongs to, and all hope of a girls' night fades away. But in its place is joy for my sister. She deserves such happiness after a hard life.

Alexis still has her back to the driveway and must not have heard the tires or engine, but her ears definitely perk up when the car door opens and her boyfriend climbs out. She turns and throws her hands onto her hips. "Dax Nyhart, what are you doing here?"

Ah, that must be why I didn't know he was coming from Los Angeles, where he moved a few months ago for work. She didn't know either.

Sunglasses on, he leans his tall frame against the car door and just smiles at her. That smile used to infuriate her when they were work enemies. Now, if the way she smiles back at him is any indication, it has quite the opposite effect.

"My work trip got canceled so I thought I'd come and surprise my woman with a visit."

"I've told you that I'm not a possession." Somehow, Alexis keeps her calm, tilts her chin up, and says with a haughty air, "And what if I'd had plans?"

He shuts the door and advances toward her with quick steps, slipping one arm around her back and plunging the other into her hair. "Then I'd make the most pathetic puppy dog eyes until you changed them." He peeks over her shoulder at me. "Hey, Kennedy."

"Hi, Dax," I say with a laugh. Scooping up my box of clothing, I move toward the open garage door. "Don't let me interrupt."

"Oh, I won't."

Just as he swoops in to kiss my sister—who has turned into a giggling machine—I walk toward Ryan's house, where I can deposit this box into my new room. Since Alexis will now be occupied, I might as well get this new life started tonight.

"Here goes nothing," I whisper before grabbing the door knob.

Of course, that's the moment when my phone rings in my back pocket. I set the box on the front stoop and reach into my back pocket.

Gran.

She must have read the text I sent this morning. And instead of texting back like a normal person, she's decided to call. I could do the super immature thing and ignore it, but this *is* my grandmother. And I'm determined to deal with problems head-on now. That's what adults do, right? So I slide my finger across the screen and hold the phone up to my ear. "Hi, Gran."

"What's this job you're going on about, Kennedy?"

No *hello*. No, *how are you, sweetie*? Gran is a special kind of grandmother—the kind who wears business slacks and a blazer instead of knit sweaters and mumus, who is in the salon chair asking for highlights in her still-blonde hair every three weeks instead of a perm.

The kind who demands more of her only granddaughter than she does of her employees. And that's saying a lot.

"Hi, Gran. Nice to hear from you." I blow out a breath and walk down Ryan's steps, out into his yard. The grass is mostly dead from our ongoing drought, but there's one little patch of blades staying strong, peeking through the ground and into the cold hard world like brave little soldiers. "How are you?"

"I'm fine, of course." I hear the clacking of keyboard keys in the background. Shouldn't be surprised that she's at work on a Saturday. The woman is a sixty-something-year-old machine. "But we're not talking about me. Why have you decided to turn down my perfectly good work opportunity? It's not even an entry-level job, Kennedy. You won't be able to get any marketing position of this caliber anywhere else in the country without a degree."

She has a point. And if the nanny gig hadn't come along, I might have been forced to consider taking Gran up on her offer. But it did. And now I don't. "And it's a very generous offer, Gran, but I like living near Alexis."

"Who at some point is probably going to move away to be with that new boyfriend of hers."

I blink. "How did you know—"

"I know all, dear. Remember, I'm richer than dirt. I have my ways."

Kicking off my shoes, I step onto the patch of living grass, relish the feel of it beneath my toes. The only thing that beats it is sand at the beach, which I really need to visit again soon. "It's a good job, Gran. I'm a nanny for the girls next door. Their uncle has them for the next six months and needed someone to watch them."

There's only silence in response, and I pull my phone away to make sure I didn't lose the connection. "Gran? You there?"

"I'm here." A deep sigh rattles from the other line. "I just needed a moment to process the fact you are turning down a marketing position—the thing you are planning to study at school, if you even plan to return like you say—in order to … babysit."

My toes curl against the ground and I shake a fist at the sky. Thank goodness this isn't a video call or she might see my curled lip too. "Gran, the neighbor is a doctor." Like Chloe said, it doesn't hurt to throw that little tidbit out there. "And he's kind of desperate for someone, and I'm good with the girls. He's paying me really well. Enough to pay for the entire first year of school."

"What's his name?"

"What?"

"The doctor. His name."

"Ryan Rosche. Why?"

More clacking and some hmms. Then, "I knew it."

I pinch the bridge of my nose. Do I even want to ask? "Knew what?"

"He's quite handsome, don't you think?"

My jaw drops. "Gran! That's … what are you talking about?"

"I looked him up. There's only one Dr. Ryan Rosche in San Diego, and his photo is on a hospital website. And oh my, yes. He's just the sort of man who might turn your head."

And I know it's something Mila would do, but I don't care. I stamp my foot. "He's not going to turn my head."

"That's what your mother said too when she went to

work for that oil and gas attorney. Remember how that turned out?"

Of course I do. After six months of dating, he dumped her for another woman—and she had to find a new assistant job. We had to find a new home too.

"And then there was that Hollywood director. He pulled the wool over her eyes for a year, didn't he? But I knew. I told Pippa that he was no good, that she'd be better off taking a job with me. But just like you, she didn't. Just like you, she let a man make her decisions for her and ruin her life."

My stomach is roiling, cutting and cruel, and I don't know if there's lava inside or ice. Maybe both, and they're destroying each other, and me in the process. Because I hear the same things in my head now as I did that time when I was ten years old, when Gran and Mom argued while I was hiding on the stairs …

No. She doesn't get to control the narrative here. Ryan didn't make any decisions for me. I'm the one in charge, going after what I want. Which is to take care of Mila and Ava, and earn enough money to put MYSELF through college.

I'm just glad I didn't tell her I was moving in with him. That would have taken this argument to a whole different level.

"Look, Gran—"

"Don't take that defensive tone with me, young lady."

I'm tempted to hit the Mute button and scream. "I'm just trying to explain myself to y—"

"No explanation needed." *Clack, clack, clack.* "But like

the loving grandmother that I am, I'll keep the marketing position open for one month. Maybe that will be long enough for you to get this man and his *job offer* out of your system." She says job offer like it's a dirty word—and all of her inferences and insinuations make me more than angry.

They make me … sad.

How can a person whose blood I share know me so little? Think so little of me?

Still, I can't afford to sneer at her counteroffer. Because what if the probation period with Ryan is up and he decides I'm not a good fit for the position anymore? That would leave me back at square one.

At that point, after such a failure, maybe Gran's offer would look more appealing.

So instead of hanging up on my grandmother and telling her what I think of her appalling behavior, I grit my teeth and say what is expected of me. "I appreciate you holding the job." But no, I'm still making a caveat. "But give me until the end of February." That would take me a few days past my probation period with Ryan, give me some wiggle room to make a decision if it comes to that.

There's a long pause, pregnant with all of Gran's favorite children: shame, guilt, calculation. "Fine. By March 1, if you haven't agreed to give up this foolishness, then I'm giving the job to someone else." She clicks off and I shove the phone back into my pocket.

Finally, I let loose the frustrated scream that's been building.

"Everything all right?"

Yelping, I turn to find Ryan leaning against the front post of his porch, watching me.

Nodding sheepishly, I march right back up the steps and reach for the box of clothes I abandoned there earlier. "Just talking with my grandma."

"Ah." He takes the box from my hands—and somehow, I don't mind. Then he props open the door with his free hand, because apparently HE only needs one hand to hold the weighted load. "How about we find something to turn that frown upside down?"

Who says that? I laugh. "Have you been watching TV shows with Mila?"

"How'd you know?"

"A wild guess." I step inside and Finley greets me with a rub against my leg—one that knocks me backward into Ryan.

"Whoa." He steadies me with a hand on my lower back. "You okay?"

The guy probably thinks I can't walk without falling over. And I'd gladly lean into it, if he wasn't now my boss. And if my grandma's words—Alexis's too—weren't ringing in my ear.

Straightening, I take back the box from him. "I'm fine."

And I am. I can do this. I *am* strong.

I will resist Dr. Ryan's Southern boy charm and do my freaking job like *I'm* the boss.

six

YOU KNOW those movies where a character is so pathetically bad at cooking and she catches pancakes on fire and the smoke alarm goes off and the dog starts barking at the ceiling and the hot man that she was trying to cook for runs out of his room with his shirt off because, well, he thinks his house is on fire and was likely asleep just a few moments before?

I am that character.

This is that movie.

And Ryan is that hot man. "What the—?"

"Hi." From my place standing on the kitchen island, I sheepishly wave a spatula splattered with lumpy pancake batter. Then I point it at the smoke detector I still can't quite reach. "Can you help?" The blare of the alarm shreds my ears.

Shouting, Mila and Ava run into the room with hands over their ears.

Like a fictional movie hero, Ryan grabs a chair,

climbs up, and easily reaches the alarm to shut it off. Silence now radiates where there was chaos.

He lowers himself to the ground and offers his hand to me. "Well, that's one way to start your first day as the newest house resident."

My face must be as red as the sweatshirt he loaned me the other night—the one that's hanging in my new closet. The one I considered wearing this morning when I crawled out of bed because of the chill clinging to the air. But I thought that might not look very professional of me. Might look a little desperate.

He's still not getting it back, though.

"Thanks," I mumble as I grab his hand and hop off the island, careful to avoid staring at defined pecs that are now conveniently—or not so conveniently—at eye level. "I was trying to make us all breakfast."

"Maybe next time just buy us donuts." With a sneer, Ava turns on her heels and stomps from the room.

"Ava, come on," Ryan calls after her. He turns to me, winces. "Sorry."

"I don't blame her for being upset. I'm sorry I woke you all up."

Mila wanders into the kitchen and peers at the plate of charred pancakes. "Miss Kenny, you don't cook very good."

"Shhh." Ryan sweeps her into his arms and moves her to the couch, then clicks on some cartoons for her to watch. After snagging a T-shirt off the couch and slipping it over his head, he returns to the kitchen and leans against the counter. "That was really nice of you, but since it's your first morning with us, how about I do the cooking, huh?"

I push a piece of hair behind my ear. "I can help."

"Hmmm, is that such a good idea?" He laughs. "How about you make us some coffee?"

I perk up. "Now that I can do." Turning to his counter, I stop, realizing something I hadn't noticed before. "Where's your espresso machine?"

"Not all of us are professional baristas." He points to the cupboard just behind my legs. "The coffee maker is under there. It's just a regular 12-cup."

"Oh, sweet, sweet Ryan." I cluck my tongue. "That's just never going to do."

"Uh oh." He picks up the bowl of batter I slopped together earlier today. It's thick and gloopy. I thought I followed the directions, but maybe I didn't add enough milk? "How about we go to the store and get you the machine you want after breakfast?"

I freeze. "Wait, what? No, I was just kidding." Squatting down, I open the cabinet door and fish out the coffee maker. Clearly the man doesn't use it often, since it's stuffed behind a blender and a food processor. "This is fine." When I stand with the coffee pot in hand, he's shucking my batter into the garbage.

And he's looking at me. "This is your home, at least for a little while. You should feel comfortable, Kennedy. If you want an espresso machine, we'll get you an espresso machine."

Who is this guy? Brooks was never this quick to agree to any changes I wanted to make to our apartment. I place the pot on the counter and turn, crossing my arms. Mila's cartoons buzz in the background. "Espresso machines are expensive. I'm fine with this."

"In case you haven't noticed"—Ryan grins at me as he takes the dirty bowl to the sink and starts washing it out—"I'm a doctor. It's not a problem."

If the same words had come out of Brooks's mouth, I'd have felt the pride smack me in the face, but I know Ryan's just teasing. He doesn't take himself so seriously. He has money, but he doesn't flaunt it. In fact, his whole house is proof of that. There isn't anything that's super new or fancy. The house is old, though kept up, and his furniture is worn but comfortable. His truck is the only thing he owns that probably cost a decent chunk of money, but it has some dents and must be a decade old at least.

And yet, he's willing to get some new-fangled coffee machine he likely won't even use after I've gone. Simply because I want it.

Tears burn the back of my eyes. How silly of me to want to cry over a coffee machine—over a guy's basic kindness—but here we are. "You can take it from my wages."

He's now mixing together a batter from scratch— flour, eggs, sugar, vanilla—and I watch his powerful hands as they whisk, making something from nothing. Flustered, I turn and move to the pantry where I find an old can of grocery-brand coffee grounds. I hold back a grimace and start adding the water and grounds to the coffee maker. Well, it's not going to be great, but I can make it a little better. I wander toward Ryan and reach around him to grab the cinnamon.

He glances down at me, surprise rimming his eyes, but I just smile and move back to the coffee.

I hear the sizzle of butter on a skillet and start humming as I add cinnamon to the coffee grounds, then snap the lid closed and hit Brew. Ha ha! Ryan's not the only doctor in this house. Still humming, I do a little shimmy and return the ground coffee to the pantry shelf. When I emerge, Ryan's standing at the stove, flipping a golden brown pancake in his T-shirt and flannel pajama pants.

And if it isn't just the most domestic and sexiest thing I've ever seen …

Professional, Kennedy.

Yep. Right.

Straightening my spine, I approach him. He's already got a whole plate of pancakes piled high, and they look delicious. "Need me to help with anything else?"

"You could get the table set and the syrup out. Maybe grab some fruit?"

"Of course."

"Ava can help if you want."

"Nah, let her sleep. It's Sunday."

He nods, one blond curl bobbing over his forehead. "Monday morning will come in hot and fast for her."

Laughing, I move to the cupboard for the plain white plates. "It's so funny how kids go from waking up at six am to sleeping until noon when they're preteens."

"Right? Then as adults, we're slaves to the schedule. And my body doesn't let me sleep past seven now anyway."

The plates are cool against my palms as I carry them to the table. "That's because you're an old man."

"You'll be here in a few years, so don't be laughing too hard." Ryan flips off the burner and gathers the plate of pancakes, carrying it to the table. "You never did tell me the other night how old you were, though you seem to think we're decades apart." He chuckles as he leans in to put the plate on the table.

"Just one."

His hand freezes under the plate and he looks at me. "One what?"

"One decade. Well, one decade plus a year."

His lips pull tight and he straightens. "Wait. How old are you?"

"Twenty-three."

And yep, I'm definitely not imagining how pale his whole face gets. He coughs. "Seriously?"

"Yeah." I shrug as if this conversation doesn't bother me, but I really don't like how he steps away from me like I'm carrying some disease he doesn't want to catch. Does he think young-itis is a thing?

"I could have sworn you were a lot older than that."

"Guess I'm mature for my age." Feeling unnaturally warm, I move to the fridge and grab out a container of washed berries, which I open and toss into a large bowl. "Besides, age is just a number, right?"

His eyebrows push together and he stares at the table. "Sure, yeah."

He's saying "sure," but his whole body is saying that age is definitely *not* just a number. And the fact he might see me differently now that he knows I'm eleven years younger than him … well, it makes me want to be super immature and dump these berries onto his head, is what.

A loud boom on the TV makes us both jump, but it's just that roadrunner running from a trap that darn coyote set for it. Mila's giggles fill the air.

I force my shoulders to relax. Ryan's reaction to my age shouldn't matter. It's not like it changes how well I'm going to take care of his nieces—and that's why I'm here, after all.

Wait. He doesn't think I'm too young to care for them properly, right?

"Ryan."

He looks up at me, opens his mouth. Shuts it.

Lowering my voice, I move toward him and put on the demeanor of someone who is sure of herself. "I am perfectly qualified to watch your nieces, but if you don't think I am, then tell me now and I'll—"

"No." He reaches out a hand as if he's going to cup my shoulder, then seems to think better of it. He takes a deep breath. "You're right. Age is just a number. I've only known you a little while, but I can already tell you have more compassion and empathy in your little finger than a lot of women ever get in their whole lifetime."

Whoa. "Um. Thanks."

"I'm just speaking the truth."

Mila giggles again, and the strain on his face melts away.

"Those girls matter more to me than anything, and you're the right person to help me take care of them. I'm so grateful you agreed to do this."

And here comes that pesky burning behind my eyes again. He believes in me more than my own family does. What does that say? That maybe he just doesn't know me well enough yet?

But it makes me want to be better. To prove to everyone that I really can do this. "I won't let you down. I promise."

seven

. . .

IT'S BEEN … a week.

A long week.

The girls are amazing, but they're still kids. So we've had our share of temper tantrums and stubbornness and tears (some of them mine). And working two jobs is a lot more physically exhausting than I thought it would be. Don't get me wrong. I don't regret this decision to become a nanny at all.

But the shiny newness of it has faded a bit. And in its place is grit and reality and the hard work of learning how to communicate with a preschooler with OPINIONS and a preteen who wants nothing to do with me.

And then there's the uncle.

Oh, the uncle.

Quite honestly, I've done my level best to avoid being around him as much as possible. Because I find that when I'm in his presence, I can't help the way my heart squeezes or my palms sweat or my eyes seems to track him like I'm a trained hunter and he's what's for dinner.

Hot mess over here, remember?

So when he gets home from work, I've been mostly slipping away into my room. And unless he's working an overnight shift, I either stay locked away there or head to Alexis's house to hang with Chloe or Shelby or my sister or whoever happens to be free. (One night, I was even so desperate as to sit on the couch in the semi-darkness while Tia the scary bodyguard cracked and crunched her way through a bag of pistachios and Chloe slept in the other room. It was not my finest moment.)

Even now, when it's early on the weekend and I know Ryan's off taking a run around the neighborhood on his day off—he texted me last night to make sure I'd be home—I peek out of my door and scurry to the bathroom down the hall for a shower. Don't want to risk an awkward run in with him alone while the girls are sleeping their Sunday morning away.

The door squeaks shut behind me and I flick on the showerhead, undress, and slip into the warm stream of water that is the perfect massage for my muscles. I haven't had time to hit one of Lauren's cycling classes in a while, yet every inch of me is aching, probably from taking Mila to the park the last few afternoons. The girl always wants me to push her on the swing until my arms practically fall off, then go on the slides with her. And lemme tell ya—those playgrounds are *not* made for adults, even petite ones.

After washing my hair with my favorite coconut shampoo, I lather up my loofa and scrub away the stress of the week. It was a lot, sure, but I also felt such a wonderful sense of purpose. I know I'm doing something important here, and the fact that it's hard only makes it more satisfying. And hey, bonus—it's kept me from having to take that job with Gran. I haven't heard from her since our chat, and that's just fine with me. I figure I have several more weeks before I have to speak to her again. (But who's counting?)

Once I step out of the shower, my feet sink into the thick, brown bathmat. Flipping over, I wind my hair up with a towel and dry off my body with another.

Then, I reach for my fresh clothing—and freeze.

Shoot.

I know I laid them out on my bed. But they're nowhere to be seen. I must have left them there.

Oh, Kennedy, you really are a mess.

Bracing myself against the counter, I consider my options. I could put my pajamas back on, but there's truly nothing worse than putting dirty clothes onto a freshly washed body. I love the refreshing snick of clean fabric sliding against clean skin. I chew my lip and unlock the door, leaning out to listen. The only sound is a clock ticking somewhere. No movement to be heard down the hall, not even Finley who sleeps in Ryan's room. Ryan probably took him on his run, anyway, and it's highly unlikely they're back yet. And even more unlikely that he'd cross my path for the five seconds I'd be in the hallway.

I'm going for it.

I fly out of the room and race down the hallway for

my open door—at the exact moment when Ryan rounds the corner in his sweat-soaked running shirt.

Oh my *oof*—we run right into each other, and his arms wrap around me protectively so I don't fall. My face is ONCE AGAIN pressed to his chest, which smells of some sort of manly deodorant and only the faintest trace of sweat. Dude. I always smell like a freaking pile of garbage after I exercise. Of course he'd smell halfway enticing.

"Are you okay?"

I nod, but stay frozen there. The towel on my head has fallen off—my wet hair tumbling free around my shoulders—and I'm afraid to look down and see whether my body towel is still secure. But I have to. This whole thing will be made infinitely worse if one of the girls comes out and finds us smooshed together like this.

Slowly, I reach my hand up between our chests, and breathe relief to find that everything essential is still covered. When I ease back out of Ryan's arms, his eyes widen with appreciation before he averts them. "Um. I'm gonna go towel off. I mean"—he mutters something under his breath—"shower off. If you're okay."

The fact he's flustered too actually makes me feel better. I release a pent-up giggle. "I'm okay."

With a nod—at the wall, not me—he heads toward his room and I head toward mine and subsequently flop onto the bed, groaning into the pillows. Seriously, what are the stinking odds? They are *not* in my favor, that's for sure.

"Just be an adult about this, Kennedy." Right. Yes. If I want him to see me as any sort of mature, then I need to handle this well. With another few deep breaths, I put on my clothes—a pair of yoga pants and an off-the-shoulder shirt that feels like silkworms just wove it—comb out my hair, and head toward the kitchen for some coffee.

Coffee makes everything better, right?

From what I can tell, the girls are still asleep so I turn on the espresso machine Ryan surprised me with earlier in the week and hum while grabbing a carton of yogurt from the fridge. No more culinary attempts by me, no sir. Once I slop some into a bowl, I make Ryan and I both an Americano, sit on one of the island stools with my cuppa and my yogurt, and wait for him to inevitably join me.

Unless it's now his turn to avoid me.

Finally, he comes out barefoot in a hooded sweatshirt and sweatpants, Finley on his heels before the dog veers for the couch and hops up. When Ryan spies the coffee I made him, his shoulders seem to relax a bit. "You didn't have to make that for me."

"Okay, I can take it back," I tease, reaching for the cup.

He swats my hand away playfully and slides onto the stool next to me before taking a sip from the mug and closing his eyes. "I'm not much of a coffee drinker, but that's magic."

"It kind of is, huh?"

We sit there in silence for a few long moments, both just drinking our coffee—though I don't think either of us needed it to wake up today. He had his run, I had my shower, and we both had our run-in.

Oh my sheesh, that was …

Don't think about it, don't think about it, don't—

"Thanks for sticking around so I could get in my run. It was nice to be out there again."

Whew. Regular conversation. This, I can do. "No problem. Though I don't know a single thing that's nice about running." I pick up my spoon and shove a bite of yogurt and granola in. The granola's crunch seems to reverberate through the entire room.

"You're not a runner, huh?" Slightly hunched over his mug, which he holds in both hands, Ryan peeks at me out of the corner of his eye. "So what's your poison? Yoga? Cycling? Pilates?"

"Nothing at the moment." When he scoffs, I lift an eyebrow. "What?"

"Nobody gets a body like *that* without—" Ryan's eyes go wide. Must have realized what he was about to say.

And I shouldn't tease him. I know I shouldn't. But it's just too easy. I lean an elbow on the counter, my face turned his way, and twirl a piece of my hair, batting my eyes and trying to look innocent. "Without what?"

Swearing under his breath, he gulps down a huge sip of coffee—and coughs.

And coughs.

I smack him on the back, but he doesn't stop. Getting up, I grab him a bottle of water from the refrigerator and bring it to him with the lid untwisted.

He guzzles it, then sets it down. "Thanks."

"No problem." I resume my spot beside him and take another bite of yogurt.

He frowns, opens his mouth, closes it. Refocuses on his coffee.

Now what?

I don't want things to ever feel awkward between us. Sure, I want to keep things professional, but that doesn't mean we can't be friendly, right? Even co-workers are friendly. (Well, most of the time … Alexis and Dax were a different story.) Teasing and opening up to him don't have to equal flirtation. They're just basic human decency.

So I choose to continue the conversation as if he hadn't blatantly revealed his attraction for me. "Actually, I used to be super into exercising. Like, I'd do yoga or Pilates every day, sometimes twice a day."

"Why so often?"

Might as well tell him now how stupid I was to stay with a guy who treated me like garbage. "Because my boyfriend always made me feel like I had to be at my absolute best." I huff out a sardonic laugh. "He wouldn't even take pictures with me unless I had my hair and makeup done."

"No way."

"Yep. And I thought that was normal. We were both social media influencers. You know, someone who shares their life publicly online and creates partnerships with brands—"

"I know what an influencer is, Kennedy." He rubs his chin, which appears super smooth. He must have shaved when he was in the shower. "I'm not *that* old."

He says it with a teasing catch in his voice, and I play with the necklace at my throat to keep myself grounded at the sudden airiness I feel in my bones. "I don't know, Old Man. You looked a little confused."

"Okay, Young'un. Whatever you say."

He's joking with me! We've officially moved past the awkwardness. I want to get up and dance and clap my hands at the light dancing in his eyes. My heart is swaying like it's freaking Ginger Rogers.

But just as soon, Ryan's expression darkens. "Just for the record, that guy's an idiot if he cared more about your appearance than your personality. Don't get me wrong—there's nothing bad anyone could say about your appearance"—*sway, sway, sway*—"but appearances fade. I hate social media's obsession with it. That's why I don't even have an account."

"I'm sorry, what? You really *are* an old man." I take another sip of warm coffee, the silky liquid sliding down my throat as I smile over my mug at him.

"Nah, I just prefer to live in reality."

"And you don't think there's reality to be found there?" Some of the most genuine people I met, I met online. Or I thought they were genuine, anyway. But when Brooks and I broke up, and he started spreading lies about me, some of them abandoned me.

"Not saying it can't." He swivels back and forth on his seat, as if it's helping him think. "I grew up in a tiny town in Oklahoma. Out in the country. People really knew each other, sometimes, when you didn't want them to." His lips curve up. "But we were a real community, and that was the beauty of growing up like that. People saw you at your best and your worst, but they didn't care. And when tragedy happened …"

"When your parents died, you mean?"

He nods. "They were really there for us. At least, until Sophie couldn't take what she called their hovering and moved us to the city."

I wait to see if he's going to say more, but he doesn't. "That must have been nice. To have a community like that, I mean. I grew up in a bit of a superficial family that's all about appearances. You should see my grandma. Even at sixty-something, she's a gorgeous force to be reckoned with. Not only that, she's smart, the CEO of a company that employs thousands of employees in San Francisco. Successful, driven …"

"But not so much loving?"

"How did you know?"

"I remember your face after you talked to her last week."

"Right." I go back to fiddling with my necklace, sighing. "I just wish she would see me for me, you know? But I think she sees my mom whenever she looks at me. Doesn't want me to make the same mistakes she did."

"What mistakes?" He shuts his eyes, grimaces. "Sorry, I didn't mean to pry."

"I don't mind telling you." Although how do you tell someone that your mom's biggest mistake might have been … you?

The necklace chain is bumpy beneath my fingers as I slide them up and down. "My mom was beautiful, smart, and talented—she was a painter. But according to Gran, she had one fatal weakness. Men."

Ryan finishes off his coffee and sets down his cup, but doesn't say anything else. Gives me room to share.

"She lived life on her terms but was never happy. She blamed the men she was with and moved from guy to guy." Including my dad—but I'm not telling Ryan about that ugly part of my life. I don't want to go *too* deep here. "And so she never really did anything on her own. Gran, on the other hand, was married once. She kept her maiden name in a time when that was kind of unheard of. And she threatened to divorce my grandpa when he didn't want her to take over her father's company. From then on, he let her do whatever she wanted."

"She sounds like a strong woman."

"She is, in a way. But I think she believes that being strong is the opposite of being soft, and that softness—an open heart—is to be despised."

"And you think differently."

I shrug. "All I know is that I wish we were closer. She and my sister are the only family I have, and neither of them really believes I'm strong enough to do things on my own." At least Alexis loves me for who I am, but my past mistakes have blinded her to what I'm really capable of.

Maybe they've blinded me too.

I blink back some tears, and Ryan's face twists. He cups my elbow gently in his rough palm. "You're strong, Kennedy. Anyone who's survived what you have and still has empathy like you do can't be considered weak."

Ugh, this man … he can't say things like that to me. Because they make me want to close the distance between us, twirl my fingers into the hair at the base of his neck, and pull his lips down to meet mine.

But that would be such a Pippa move, it's not even funny.

And I'm. Not. Her.

I really hope I'm not, anyway.

eight

· · ·

I REMEMBER how rough the preteen and teen years can be.

Trying not only to find yourself and figure out what *you* like—not just what will keep you off the "not cool" list at school, but what you actually are drawn to, what makes you come alive. Navigating all the hormones and body changes and uncertainties and girl drama without completely losing your mind.

Add family drama on top of that? Plus the inability to really and truly change your circumstances because, hi, you're still not an adult?

Yeah. I remember. Rough doesn't even come close to describing it.

Heck, sometimes I still feel like a teenager in a twenty-three-year-old's body. Which is why, even though it's four o'clock on Wednesday afternoon and I just worked all day at the coffee shop and am exhausted, I'm not reacting to the barrage of insults being thrown my way.

Even though I'm pretty sure Ava wants me to.

"I told you, I don't *need* a nanny." She screams the words from across the kitchen island, her face red, her blonde hair streaming down her back. "*We* don't need you. I can watch my sister myself. Why don't you just go home?"

Mila's in the corner, hugging her knees, her face buried in the crevice between them. I can tell by her shaking shoulders that she's crying. This is one of those moments when I feel completely inadequate to be a care provider. Surely professionals have methods of dealing with yelling preteens and teary-eyed preschoolers, especially when they're occurring at the same time. And yet, even with a chat earlier this week with their social worker about ways to handle these kinds of meltdowns, I'm frozen, afraid that comforting Mila will somehow make Ava feel even worse and run back to her room.

At least now Ava's talking (well, yelling) instead of stuffing it all inside. It's good for her to release those emotions, but this isn't really the best way to do it. If only I could channel that energy, that anger, into something productive.

"Your uncle hired me, Ava." My mind whirls with possible responses, and that one feels so lame. But how do I get through to this girl? She won't let any of us in. And I get it. I really do. Her mother—the one person she should be able to count on—left her. Even if she didn't choose jail exactly, she chose alcohol over her daughters. And even though alcoholism is a disease, an addiction, surely all Ava can see is how that choice has taken her mom away from her and her sister.

"Well, he can unhire you for all I care!"

Mila whimpers. Groaning, I move toward her, squat, and stroke her hair. She immediately opens her eyes and throws herself into my arms. "I don't like it when she gets this way."

"She's just upset." I peek up at Ava, who looks slightly chagrined for a split second, but then throws her arms over her chest and huffs.

"Ugh, whatever." Then she begins the long stomp to her room.

But no. We can't keep going like this. If she goes back to that manly, uninspired room again—

Wait. That's it. "Ava, stop." My words come out clipped, almost harsh. I soften my tone. "Please."

She stills, her back to me, and glances over her shoulder. "What do you want?"

To keep myself from responding with just as snarky of an attitude, I breathe through my nose and stand, pulling Mila to her feet. "I need to run a little errand. And I'd like for you to come with us."

Ava turns and faces me full on. She plants her feet shoulder width apart, like she's cementing herself to the tile floor. "I can stay home alone," she spits out. "I'm not a baby."

I hold up my hand. "I know. But I need your help with this errand. In fact"—I cock my head—"I literally can't do it without you." Leaning down, I whisper in Mila's ear and ask her to go get her shoes on. "Then you can grab a lollipop for the car ride over."

Smiling, she skips off, all tears forgotten.

Meanwhile, Ava's eyes have narrowed. "What's the errand?"

"You'll find out once we're in the car."

"You can't make me go."

"You're right." There's no way I'm strong enough to wrestle her into my car, and I wouldn't want to anyway. This is a surprise I think she'll like, but she has to choose it too. She's got to meet me halfway, here. "But you won't know what I've got planned unless you come."

Five minutes later, we're all in the car. Ava's scowling with earbuds in, but she's there beside Mila, who has already fallen asleep. Preschool must have worn her out earlier today. Lifting a prayer that Ryan will be okay with this (maybe I should have checked with him first) and that this will actually work, I slap on the radio and drive to the steady beat of T Swift.

When we finally pull up to the hardware store, I look in the rearview mirror. Ava's staring at the sign, nose scrunched. She's clearly confused but she doesn't ask me what we're doing here. Maybe she's too proud. But I know even if she does so begrudgingly, she'll follow me inside because she wants to find out what's going on. I get out of the car and lean in to unbuckle Mila, who starts to yawn and wake up as soon as I take her into my arms.

Ava gets out on her side and together the three of us leave behind the cold crispness of a cloudy afternoon for the warmth and false lighting of the store. The air smells of sawdust as we make our way toward the back. I've never been to this particular store, but the layout is similar to that of others I've been to, and the signs point me to where I want to go.

Before I know it, we're standing in front of hundreds of paint swatches, which make a vibrant rainbow on the wall. Mila is fully awake now, running up to various swatches and ooo-ing about which is the prettiest. I turn to Ava, who's standing there, staring. "Go ahead. Pick which one you want for your room."

Her jaw slackens. "For my …?"

I nod, moving forward. "You wear lots of pinks and purples, but I'm guessing you wouldn't want your wall that color. Of course, I could be wrong, and that's cool. It's all up to you."

"It is?" She takes one step, slow and careful, like she's honestly afraid the floor will turn to quicksand. Then she steps back, shakes her head. "I don't think Uncle Ryan will be cool with this."

I don't want to lie and say I've gotten his permission, but there is one assurance I can most definitely give her that's a hundred percent honest. "He loves you and wants you to feel at home. If this helps you do that, then I'm sure he'll be cool with it."

"Really?"

Two older women arrive at the wall and begin exploring the colors. They're focused on the oranges, so I head for the blues. After perusing for a few moments, I select a blue that's got a purplish tint, pulling loose the sample swatch card and holding it up so Ava can see. "If I were to pick a color for my room, this would be it right here. Blues are known to calm people, and I've got a lavender bedspread, so this would match really well. Plus I could accent with some other blues if I wanted." I pause. "What do you think?"

I can almost see the invisible force that's tugging her toward me. She wants to give in—I can tell by the way her lips twitch, her fingers curl into balls at her sides, her knees bend. But she's resistant to the principle of doing anything I ask of her. So I wait, keeping an eye on Mila, who is now sitting at a display dining room table and chairs right beside the paint sample wall, coloring in the activity book I brought along and humming happily to herself while she twirls a lollipop in her mouth.

The old ladies leave, and a pregnant young couple approaches, discussing the perfect color for their baby nursery.

And still I wait. But instead of looking at the ground, Ava is now studying the wall, even if from afar—so this is progress.

My phone buzzes in my purse, and I pick it up. A text from Ryan: *Headed home in the next hour. Should I grab dinner on my way back?*

I have to giggle at his old man way of using punctuation so properly. But ooo, yes, good idea. Because if things go well here with Ava, I'll be too occupied to throw something edible together when we get home. I text back a thumbs-up emoji, along with a pizza emoji and a begging face GIF before stuffing my phone back into my bag.

When I look up, Ava is at the wall, pulling loose a sage green card. She bites her lip, holds up the card to look at it from all angles, then carries it to me. "This one."

Her voice might be monotone, but her eyes are sparking with something I haven't seen from her yet—life. And maybe excitement too?

So I take the card from her and ask her to watch her sister for a few minutes. Then I find an associate, ask for a gallon of the paint color, and wait while he goes to the back room to mix it up. While he's doing that, I grab a cart, some paintbrushes, tape, and all the other supplies we need.

An hour later, we're in Ava's room, all the furniture pushed to the middle of the room and covered in plastic. I managed to wrangle a ladder from Ryan's garage, and we've got some hot new band that Ava loves blaring from her cell phone. Mila, who was excited about the prospect of painting but got bored about ten minutes into setup, is playing Barbies in her room, so it's just Ava and me there together as I pry open the lid to the paint and pour it into the pan.

The chemical aroma smells like hours of my childhood, like warm afternoons cooped up in my bedroom alone, like aggressions surrendered and emotions spent.

Shaking off the memories, I pick up a paint roller and offer it to her. "You get the first roll."

She backs away like I'm trying to hand her a spider. "I don't know how."

"You don't know how to fling color onto a wall?"

A head shake.

I smile. "I'm just teasing. It's really easy, and hard to mess up. And another bonus." Pushing the roller into the paint, I get it nice and saturated before letting the loose paint fall off and shoving the long handle back into her hands. "It's therapeutic. Trust me. When I was a teenager, I painted my room more times than I could count."

"Your mom was cool with that?"

I shrug. "She wasn't home enough to notice. Always out with her latest boyfriend."

Ava frowns, but takes the rod from me. Then, she approaches the wall, lifts the paint, dabs a tiny amount on the stark white—and backs away quickly. Paint dribbles from the roller onto the plastic-covered ground. "That looks terrible."

She's right. It's a drippy smudge. But I just smile and gently take the paint roller from her, pressing the roller against the wall and smoothing out the drips. "The lovely thing about painting is that you can fix your mistakes. It's very forgiving. Here." I hold out the rod once more. "Try again."

Ava huffs out a breath and takes it, then marches forward with a determined stride. She studies the wall for a moment before rolling a long strip of paint onto the wall. The color is soft but striking. It'll look even better with two coats.

She's chosen well.

I tell her as much and she turns to me, the tiniest smile appearing at the corner of her lips. "I did, didn't I?"

"You really did."

The masculine voice makes both of us turn. I move to Ava's phone to turn down the music a little as Ryan steps inside the room in his green scrubs. His eyes are a bit red—he's coming off a twenty-four-hour shift that went long—but that doesn't stop the joy from shining through. "What are you ladies up to?"

Ava is frozen, a sculpture on ice, her gaze darting between Ryan and me.

I pat her shoulder. "We thought it was time Ava claimed the room as her own." *And you'd better not say anything against it, Ryan Rosche.*

As if he can hear my unspoken thought, his eyes crinkle at the corners. "That's a great idea. I should have thought of it."

"Really?" Ava squeaks.

"Of course. And maybe …" He tilts his head. "Maybe you could use another set of hands?"

Ugh, this guy. He's clearly dead on his feet—he has to be—and yet he's offering to help his niece paint her room. How am I supposed to keep my heart around him? His kindness isn't even aimed at *me*, but it affects me all the same.

I feel Ava's body shudder under my hand, and I give her a squeeze, hoping she will hear what I'm not saying. *It's okay to let it out.* Squeeze. *You aren't alone.* Squeeze. *We see you, and we care.*

A tear falls down her cheek. She turns to brush it away.

My eyes find Ryan's. He mouths "Thank you" and I swear my cheeks feel sunburned and chapped. I just nod and release Ava. "Well, I guess I'll go see what Mila's doing."

"She's already eating the pizza I brought home. There's more on the counter."

"Bless you." I walk past Ryan and nod for him to follow me into the hallway.

He does, but before I can say anything, he leans in and swipes his thumb over my cheekbone, a caress that leaves a popping trail of fire behind. I can't help but lift my fingers to rub the heat away. Blinking, I try desperately to remember why we are standing here together.

"Sorry," he says. "You had some paint there."

Paint. Right. "Um, thanks." I lower my voice. "So, I probably should have asked if you were okay with us doing this, but I just wanted to find a way to connect with Ava."

"Of course I don't mind. I would never have thought of it, but it's brilliant." He leans against the wall. "*You're* brilliant."

Gah. "Yeah, well, thanks for letting her do this. It means a lot to her—to claim this space as her own. I can tell."

"I'd do anything for her."

"I know you would."

He studies me for a few moments longer before responding. "I'd do anything for *anyone* in my circle."

Is he implying that *I'm* in that circle?

STAHP it, Kennedy. It doesn't matter.

Blinking, I take a step away. Because what else can I do? He could so easily become my sun, my everything. If I stay here, I'm bound to be drawn into his orbit. But I have to stick to my own.

"Have fun painting." I force a smile. "I need to go check on Mila."

"Right." His smile wobbles and he clears his throat. "You know where to find me if you need me."

"I know." *But I won't.* Then I turn and head for the kitchen, aware with every step that he's still watching me go.

I should be in bed. Asleep. That's what all rational people who will inevitably have a four-year-old pouncing on their head at six a.m. the next morning do.

But nope. After getting Mila into the bath and then bed, checking on Ryan and Ava's painting progress (the room looks fabulous and Ava was so happy), and eating some ice cream next door with Alexis (who spent the whole time trying to convince me that I should quit my new job and move "home"), I don't care what's rational.

It's eleven p.m. and I'm snuggled up under a blanket on the couch watching reruns of *The Bachelor.*

Finley's lying on the overstuffed chair snoring the late evening away, both girls are asleep, and Ryan is tucked away in his room, presumably sleeping. I haven't seen him since he finished up with Ava. Judging by the fact there's still half a pizza leftover, I don't think he ever came out and ate.

Enough thinking about your boss, Kennedy. He can do what he wants.

My finger twitches, sending the volume up one more notch. The large mounted screen flickers in the dark, and the blond male lead flies with one of twenty-something gorgeous women in a helicopter overlooking Glacier National Park in Montana. The sunlight reflects off the ice, taking me away from here.

Although now that I look at him closely, the lead kind of resembles a certain man I know in real life. He's even got a touch of a Southern accent …

"What's this?"

My head swivels and my finger jams the Pause button.

Ryan's standing on the other side of the couch, his gaze taking in the TV, lips pulled back in amusement.

"Nothing." It's not that I'm exactly embarrassed by my choice in entertainment, even though Brooks made fun of me for my love of reality television. *"It's so childish, Kennedy. None of it's real."*

Of course it's not real. No one watches it because they want reality—as ironic as that is, given the name. People watch it because it immerses them in drama that's not of their own making, taking them away from their *own* reality.

Some people might watch it, for example, because they're kinda sorta falling for their boss even though they know they shouldn't.

Ahem. I tilt my chin upward, defending my choice against what I'm sure is coming. After all, Ryan is even older and more actually mature than Brooks. He's sure to think less of me. But he just turns his eyes on me, and despite the dim lighting, I catch a sparkle.

"Looks like *something* to me." His hair is wet and even from here I can smell his woodsy shampoo.

Oh, just kill me now. If this wasn't his house, I'd demand he leave. Immediately.

But I can't exactly do that. This isn't the first time I've watched TV at night, but it's the first time he's ever been awake for it. And we never really established the rules of me using the common areas. Maybe he wants to watch something himself. After all, he's off tomorrow. Maybe this is how he unwinds and I'm standing in the way of that.

Grabbing the remote, I hold it out to him. "Did you want to watch something?"

"I just came to grab some of that pizza if any is left."

"Oh, yeah." I toss the blanket aside and stand. "I'll grab you some."

"You don't have to do that."

I'm already halfway to the kitchen by the time he protests, and I've got the fridge open and the pizza box in hand when he makes it to my side. Closing the fridge door, I straighten and realize just how close he's standing. Oh my sheesh, if I could bottle the look of him— white T-shirt stretched across his chest and broad shoulders, basketball shorts, wet hair that's elongating his curls, a bit of green paint still on his nose and evidence of how much he loves his niece—I'd be a freaking millionaire.

Because every woman would want a glimpse of what I'm selling.

But not me. Nope.

Okay, fine. I might want it, but my mom wanted all

sorts of things that weren't good for her ultimately. Surely in the moment, though, they seemed good. Amazing, even.

I shove the pizza box against his stomach. "Here."

He grunts but takes it. "Thanks."

We stand there staring at each other for a moment before I gather my senses. Maybe I should just go to bed. But I'd only lie there, blinking at the ceiling and wishing for a distraction, so I might as well get that distraction out here in the open. Biting my lip, I turn and grab a plate from the cabinet. Set it on the counter. "Enjoy your dinner."

"Thank you, Kennedy."

The way he says my name here in the dark kitchen makes me want to utterly melt. It's like sweet chocolate tossed with a bite of ginger. Decadent, smooth, and as dangerous to my heart as dessert is to my hips.

I hurry from the kitchen and plop down onto the couch. Finley raises his head, but seeing no threat, settles back down. I'm about to turn the TV back on when Ryan sits down beside me. And sure, there's some cushion between us, but I can feel the warmth of him still. "This seat taken?"

"Um. No."

"So, what are we watching?"

I can't help but chuckle. "We?"

"Well, sure. Why not?"

"Okay." I toss the remote to him. "What do you want to watch?"

He picks up a slice of cold pizza and nods toward the screen. "Whatever you're watching is fine."

I snort. "You a fan of *The Bachelor*?"

"What's that?"

"Seriously, Old Man?"

He winks at me. "Just kidding. You know it first started when I was in high school, right? Lots of the girls I knew loved it." Then he clicks on the show.

Within seconds, the couple starts to kiss.

Because of course they do.

Ryan starts to cough and takes a big swig of his water. It's adorable and I have to bite back a giggle. Eventually, he gets himself under control and, pizza crust in hand, waves it at the TV. "Okay, so who are these people?"

"You really want to know?"

He shrugs. "Sure, why not?"

And, not for the first time, I am struck by just how different this man is from my ex. Not just in looks and mannerisms, but in all the ways that matter.

I spend a few minutes giving him the rundown. "That woman is my favorite. That one is kind of trashy and just wants a hookup. That one is drama with a capital D. That one …" And on and on I go.

And he's tracking with all of it. Some might even say he's invested in it. He laughs when I laugh, and when I gasp at a particularly egregious piece of misconduct on one woman's part, his eyes go wide in mock indignation. "She didn't just do that."

"But she did! If I had some popcorn right now, I'd toss it at the screen."

He laughs and pauses the show. "I can go pop you some."

"No, no, it's okay. I should go to bed soon anyway."

"Yeah, I probably should too." Taking his last bite of pizza, he groans and places one hand against his flat stomach. "Oh man, I didn't realize how hungry I was."

"That's because you haven't eaten since lunch, I'm guessing."

He winces.

I turn in my seat, putting one leg up on the couch between us. "You *did* eat lunch, right?"

"I might have forgotten it in the fridge."

"Again?" It's not the first time he's run out the door without it. "But you have a cafeteria, right?"

"Yeah, it's just a few floors away, but I never get a chance to sneak down there. Inevitably we get a trauma patient right when it's time for my break and ..." Ryan shrugs.

He doesn't talk much about his job. I want to ask more, but his yawn makes me stop.

"Well, I know how tired you were. And hungry," I say instead. "But it was really great of you to spend your evening with Ava."

"She didn't say much at first, but started to talk about halfway through. Not about anything super significant—and I didn't pry—but it was so great to see a glimpse of the real Ava again. I've missed her."

Something like pride canters through my chest. Not a haughty pride. Not one that makes this all about me. More like, a knowing pride. One of assurance. That feeling you get when you know you did something well. Something right. A reminder that you are capable, even when others tell you differently.

"Got any other great ideas knocking around in that brain of yours?" He's still looking at the frozen TV, but I feel the heat of his gaze just as strongly as if he were staring straight into my eyes.

"N-no." Now it's my turn to cough. I take a drink of my lemon-infused sparkling water on the side table. "Ideas like that just come to me in the moment."

"Hmm." He sets down his empty plate on the coffee table and stretches his arms behind his head, closing his eyes. "Does your inspiration come from *The Bachelor*?" A smile flicks across his lips.

With a laugh, I grab one of the decorative pillows between us and smack him across the stomach with it. Before I can haul back and hit him again, he secures it with one hand and holds it there to his chest—his eyes still closed.

But that's no problem. I find another pillow that's fallen to the ground and go for his pretty boy face this time, lunging out of my seat to get some leverage. At just the right moment, his eyes open and he wastes no time in snatching me with his free hand and hauling me toward him. Wriggling free, I fall beside him onto the couch and scooch until my upper back hits the couch arm. Before I can sit up fully and gain the upper hand, he crawls over and starts to tickle my sides with abandon.

Squealing, I push on his chest with my hands but his face only comes closer to mine. Somewhere in the background, Finley barks, but I'm too far in to give up now. I push and wrestle, trying to get upright, but I can't. And yet, I know that if I truly wanted to, I could just ask.

But I don't want to.

Oh my sheesh, I *really* don't want to.

But I pretend I do, grabbing at Ryan's strong hands and pulling—to no avail. He captures both of my hands in one of his and pins them over my head. This guy's got me beat in more ways than one.

Our breathing is labored, gasping with laughter, as Ryan lowers his mouth to my ear. "Say uncle."

"No way." I giggle some more. "You're not *my* uncle."

Aaaaaand crud. That sounded far more flirtatious than I meant it to.

He pauses, and I am keenly aware of his right hand on the bare skin of my waist where my shirt must be riding up. His thumb glides across the side of my stomach, and I shiver. Hot and cold—it all spreads up and out, everywhere at once.

Then Ryan blinks, and his gaze flicks down to my lips. "No. I'm not."

I've watched enough reality TV to know that look. This man is about to kiss me, our determination to keep things professional out the window. Kaput. Unless I stop it.

I have to stop it.

His mouth begins to lower toward mine.

"We should finish," I sputter.

He freezes. "What?" His eyebrows get closer together.

"The episode." I move to sit up, and he's off of me in a flash, running his hand through his hair. Blinking at me, like he can't believe what just happened. What almost happened.

Yeah, well, get in line, buddy.

My hands fumble for the remote, which has fallen to the ground. "I-I can't wait to see what happens next."

"Oh, right. Yeah. Me either."

Then, after clearing his throat, he whistles for Finley and pats the now-empty spot on the couch between us. And I've never been so thankful for that big mutt of a dog in all my life.

nine

. . .

THERE'S nothing worse than being single on Valentine's Day, especially when it's also your birthday. But it's made a bazillion times worse when your supposed friend won't stop badgering you.

Ugh. I never should have told Chloe about what happened last week.

"I fail to see the problem, here."

"Seriously, Chlo?" I wave at Mila from my spot on the playground bench. She's made a friend—a cute little redhead boy with two missing front teeth—and is happily racing up the steps and down the slide over and over again. "I nearly kissed my boss."

Dressed in leggings, an oversized pink sweater, knee-high boots, and white designer sunglasses, my friend pivots in her seat beside me. "Sounds like *he* nearly kissed you."

"And I nearly let him." I've replayed the scene in my brain a thousand times over the last six days, but I haven't given us a chance to repeat it in person. Thankfully, due to a co-worker being out sick, Ryan's had mostly overnight shifts since then. It hasn't been great for his time with the girls, but it's been good for me to gain a little distance. A little perspective. A chance to remind myself why I need to stay focused, not swayed by his gorgeous smile and quiet sense of humor that leaves me breathless.

Not to mention his touch …

"Again, I'm not really seeing the problem here." Chloe holds up her pointer finger. "First of all, you're both single, consenting adults." Another finger joins the first. "Second of all, he's a physician. Third of all, he's a smashingly *sexy* physician."

I push her shoulder. From her spot leaning against a nearby tree, Tia shakes her head at me. I'm surprised she doesn't slice her finger across her throat in a silent threat because, GASP, I dared to touch the princess of Kentonia.

Chloe sees her bodyguard and rolls her eyes. "Ignore her. She's so hardcore sometimes."

Laughing, I make a show of putting my hands back in my lap and away from Chloe. Then I sober. "As smashingly sexy as Ryan might be, he's also my boss."

"Only for six months."

"But I don't know where I'll be after those six months are up. Maybe I'll be starting college. Could be in San Diego, but I don't know. That's the point." I shrug. "And for all I know, Ryan will decide we need to go our separate ways in a few weeks."

"That's when the probation period is up?"

"Yeah. And if he decides it's not working out for some reason"—an unlikely possibility, but you never know—"then I might have to take Gran up on her offer after all and move to San Francisco."

"You don't really want that, do you?"

"Not even a little." I keep my eyes fixed on Mila, who is now digging in the sand using some other child's toys. She's chattering like a songbird. "But I don't know. Maybe I should consider Gran's offer even if Ryan doesn't end our agreement early. Maybe *I* should be the one to say this nannying gig isn't working out."

"Except you love it."

"I do. I really do." Even though it's been much harder than I thought to keep my distance from Ryan. To not fall for him. "But maybe I shouldn't be so quick to pass up the opportunity Gran is giving me."

"Kennedy, do you even want to go into marketing? You seem more suited to something that helps people do more than sell their products. You're a bleeding heart if ever I saw one." She winks at me.

I want to laugh, but what she says stirs something in me. She's right. Completely. I would love to do something with my life that makes a difference in the world. That's probably why I'm finding this nanny job so fulfilling. Ava and Mila need someone to love on them when their uncle can't, and I feel so privileged to do so.

But I'm barely qualified to be a nanny, much less do anything else to change the world. Perhaps it's simply enough to touch as many as I can in my life outside of work.

I don't know how to say all of that to Chloe, so

instead, I'm as honest as I can be. "The idea of being stuck behind a desk day in and day out *does* make me shudder. But marketing is a solid career choice, right?" And one that would prove my competency. My "adultness."

"I still think you'd hate it," Chloe says.

"But isn't that what adulting is? Doing things you might not like in order to become the person you want to be?"

"If that's true, then I was an adult when I was five." Chloe sticks out her tongue as if she's tasted something disgusting. "The point is, Kennedy, this is your life. You get to decide what you want to do—*and* who you want to be with."

"I thought we were talking about my job."

"The subjects of your job and your dating life are rather tied up in each other at the moment."

I groan. "I know. And that's the problem. It didn't go so well for me the last time my career was tied up in my boyfriend."

My friend pulls down her designer sunglasses. "Maybe not, but it seems to me that your good doctor is quite the opposite of—what do you and Alexis call him? Stooks?"

"Yep. Stupid Brooks." A breeze blows through my hair, and I pull my jacket tighter. "I just don't want to jump into something recklessly. It's only been three months since we broke up."

"True, but did you really love the man? Like, honestly love him?"

"I thought I did."

"But have you thought about him, pined for him? Checked his social media because you want to know what he's up to?"

I consider her question. "No, actually. None of the above. Not since right around Christmas time." That was when I decided to give up social media influencing. My numbers had tanked thanks to Brooks's assertions that I wasn't who I said I was—that I was just a woman riding his coattails who'd known nothing of the "high life" until he introduced it to me.

For a month, my DMs had been filled with hate, with threats. Mostly women who couldn't believe I'd treated an "amazing man like Brooks" so poorly. I'd built my life around this "job"—around him—and when I'd gone against something he wanted, he dumped me. And it was all gone.

"So you're over him. Some breakups take a long time to heal. Others don't, especially when it was the wrong guy. And sometimes, it's the right guy and you never even get to be with him." Her eyes widen, as if she didn't mean to say that last part. Before I can open my mouth to ask her WHO exactly she's talking about, she plows onward. "The point is, I believe Brooks is your past. Maybe Dr. Ryan is your future—if you can just get past the fear of making another mistake and start trusting yourself again."

Heat pricks the back of my eyes. I can't deny there's some truth to what Chloe is saying. And maybe being with Ryan wouldn't be irresponsible if he wasn't my boss.

But he is.

Chloe and I sit there and shoot the breeze for another half hour before she checks her phone and sees a message from Lauren. "Ah, poor girl. Flutterbum strikes again."

"Flutterbum?"

She waves her hand in the air. "It's what we lovingly call Felicia Butterflum, the royal wedding coordinator back home. She's got all these ideas that Lauren doesn't want to adhere to for the wedding, but feels she has no choice." Chloe stands, and I stand with her. "Anyhow, I'd best go calm her down." When my friend leans in for a hug and a cheek kiss—she's so royal and Kentonian!—I find myself wanting to cry again.

Because only true friends tell you things you don't want to hear. And somehow, in the last place I expected to, when all the people I *thought* were my friends had abandoned me, I found a true one.

"Thank you, Chlo." I sniffle and squeeze her so tight that I'm pretty sure Tia is growling a few feet away. "Thanks for being my friend."

Chloe pulls back. "And thank you for being mine. You've made my time in America a thousand times better. Oh, and happy birthday. I hope you do something fun tonight." She waggles her perfectly curved eyebrows suggestively.

I roll my eyes again, but before I can retort, a blonde-haired tornado slams into my legs. "Miss Kenny, I hafta go potty nooooooow."

Laughing, I ruffle her hair, which is in tangles thanks to the wind. This child is going to need a bath when we get home. "Guess that's our cue to leave too."

And my cue to get re-focused on what really matters right now. Not my single status, or even my feelings over turning another year older and not having any more answers than I did last year.

No, what really matters right now? My job. And the Rosche girls.

We hurry to the bathrooms, and while Mila is using the facilities, Gran calls. We haven't communicated at all since our chat two and a half weeks ago, when she issued her ultimatum. But it *is* my birthday. She usually texts me but perhaps this year, she's decided to extend an olive branch of sorts and put more effort into wishing me well.

"Hello?"

"Are you sleeping with him yet?"

What the— "I'm sorry, you must have the wrong number."

"Kennedy Montgomery Matkin, you do not hang up the phone on your grandmother. Show some respect."

I'm the one who needs to show respect? "You know what—"

Thankfully, before I can hurl my own insults, Mila comes out of the stall and hops up onto the stepping stool to wash her hands. I tell Gran I'll have to call her back, then hang up so I can help Mila and calm myself down too.

"Miss Kenny?" Mila says after drying her hands. "You look like you need a hug." Then this precious girl wraps her arms around me and I squat to her level and return the favor. Her sweet face pulls back, smiles at me. "Feel better?"

"I do. Thank you, baby."

"I'm not a baby."

I laugh. "No, you're not." We walk hand in hand back toward the playground. "You can play for ten more minutes and then we need to head home, all right?"

She shoots me two thumbs up and races back to her little redhead.

My phone starts buzzing again in my back pocket. I know who it is. And it's my birthday. I shouldn't have to answer it, right? Birthdays are supposed to be days you do whatever the heck *you* want to do.

But I know she'll only continue to call, and what I really want is for this conversation to be over. So I answer. "Please don't tell me you called just to insult me again."

"Why dear, I didn't mean to insult you. Though I must say, I'm rather concerned that you didn't answer my question. Some might think that you're deflecting."

I grit my teeth and pace in front of the park bench, making sure to keep my eyes on Mila. "No, I am not sleeping with him," I hiss. Don't want the other nannies and parents at the park to overhear my quite inappropriate conversation. "We haven't even kissed."

"But you want to."

Argh! This woman is infuriating. "It doesn't matter. I haven't."

She sighs with more dramatics than the soap opera my mom used to love. "Perhaps you'd better take me up on my offer after all. You only have fifteen more days until I post the job description and am flooded with applications."

"Is that why you really called? For an update? Well, I don't have one. I'm still considering my options." Though if this conversation has reminded me of anything, it's that being beholden to my grandmother for anything would probably be a terrible idea.

"While I'm thrilled to hear that, I actually called for a different reason."

I plop onto the empty bench. "And what's that?"

"To wish you happy birthday, of course. So. Happy birthday."

"Oh. Um, thank you."

"You're welcome." Silence stretches and bends between us. I glance at the phone to see if I've lost the call, but the time keeps ticking away. "Well, I guess that's it."

I guess it is. Why does that make me want to sigh? Maybe because, for all her faults, Mom always made a big deal out of my birthdays. Since it was Valentine's Day, she'd volunteer for my class parties, bringing the biggest cupcakes imaginable (they were purchased, of course—I inherited my mother's skills in the kitchen). If I didn't have school, we'd spend the whole day together, shopping, sightseeing, watching movies.

Just us girls.

But now, *this* is my birthday. *This* is my family. I don't fault Alexis for having plans with Dax. I'm thrilled that she's finally with a good guy. But would it kill Gran to take a few minutes to ask me about my job, my life?

It's like she doesn't really want to know me at all.

And maybe that's true. If I didn't share her Montgomery blood, she'd have no interest in me whatsoever.

As it is, the only thing she cares about is reshaping me into someone I'm not.

But in order to avoid that, I'd have to know who I AM.

Wait. I know who I am. I'm the girl who is gonna be alone on her birthday. Again.

ten

. . .

MAYBE IT'S a lame way to spend a birthday, but I've decided to look forward to a quiet evening in bed watching reality TV on my computer and eating a tub of Ben & Jerry's Half Baked. If it's something I choose to be happy about, it's less lame, right?

But it'll still be a few more hours before my date with myself. Ava's just arrived home from school and I'm at the kitchen table helping her with her literature homework. Since painting her room last week, she seems friendlier. Still quiet, still hormonal at times, but not as surly. Possibly … happier? A few days ago, she even asked me about how I'd handle a situation with a friend. And the eye rolling has been kept to a minimum.

Meanwhile, Mila's on the couch putting a variety of hats and bows on Finley's head. The dog is sitting still like a freaking saint, even though I can hear the thump of his tail and see the twitch of his nose. He's aching to be set free from his Stay position, but he's being such a good boy.

My phone rings on the table beside me and I glance at the screen only to see Ryan's number requesting a video chat.

And there goes my stomach fluttering like it's filled with leaves about to be carried away by the wind. "Girls, it's your uncle." I turn and position the phone so he'll be able to see both girls and me in the background, then click the button to answer. "Hey, Ryan."

"Hey, y'all. How's everyone doing?" He's in his truck, but without a seatbelt, so I'm guessing he's sitting in the parking lot at work.

"Uncle Ryan, Uncle Ryan, guess what?" Mila runs right up to the phone and smudges her face against the screen. Laughing, I pull it back a tad so Ryan doesn't have to look up her nose.

"What is it, Sweetpea?"

"It's Miss Kenny's birthday!"

How did she—? My jaw tightens. I definitely didn't tell her, so she must have overheard Chloe today at the park.

Ryan's eyes turn to where I'm sitting in the corner of the screen. "Is it really? Hmm. And does Miss Kenny have plans?"

"She said she's gonna watch TV and eat ice cream."

My cheeks warm. Now, not only does he know it's my birthday—which calls attention once again to the age gap between us that seemed to make him uncomfortable—but he now also knows the depths of my lameness. Lamity? Whatever. I force a chuckle. "What can I say? I'm low maintenance."

He clucks his tongue. "Well, I was just calling to see if I could bring something home for dinner, but now I have a better idea."

Ava's head pops up with sudden interest. "What?"

"How about you ladies get dressed to go out so we can treat Miss Kennedy to a night on the town?"

"Oh, you really don't have to do that." I bite my lip. "All the restaurants will be booked up for Valentine's Day."

"Don't worry about it. I've got it handled." He rubs his chin. "I'll be home in fifteen and will just need a quick shower. Y'all get ready now and we can leave by five. Sound good?"

Mila jumps up and down, clapping. Even Ava has a smile on her face. Am I the only one who isn't happy about this turn of events?

Okay, objectively speaking, the fact a man wants to take me out for my birthday is huge. Last year, Brooks was out of town for my birthday for a guys' weekend, even when I told him how special I thought birthdays were. Especially ones on Valentine's Day. But Brooks wanted a guys' weekend, so I spent the night—you guessed it—watching TV and eating ice cream.

But remember. This year, I was going to CHOOSE it.

Instead, this amazing guy is offering to take me out, and I can't disappoint the expectant look on his face— the one that says he just wants to do something nice for the girls and me. And the girls are actually excited about something. After all they've been through, I'm not going to be the one to take that away. "What should I wear?"

"Whatever you want, but the place I'm thinking of is a bit dressier. Not super formal, but maybe somewhere in between that and casual?"

Does that mean I get to see him in something other than scrubs or pajama pants? I mean, I love that look on him, but the thought of dress pants, a dress shirt, a tie … maybe even a jacket?

Okay, now it's time for a cold, COLD shower.

"S-sounds good," I manage.

After saying goodbye, Ryan clicks off the phone and I rush to find Mila something appropriate to wear. Ava's got her clothing handled—sometimes I think the girl has more natural fashion sense than I do—and once I pull out a pink dress for Mila (it IS Valentine's Day, after all) and help her into it, comb her hair, and send her to play with her dolls, I hear Finley's mad dash toward the front door, which means Ryan's home.

Sure enough, on my walk to my room, I catch sight of him disappearing into his. I quickly select an outfit—I can't overthink this because IT IS NOT A DATE—and head toward the hall bathroom for a shower. By the time I've got my hair done, my makeup applied, and my favorite little black dress with four-inch heels tugged on to help me in the height department, it's five fifteen. Hopefully Ryan's not the kind of guy to get cranky or complain that I took too long to get ready. I experienced enough of that for a lifetime with Brooks.

For good measure, I check my appearance one more time in the full-length mirror. The backless dress hugs my curves and ends several inches above my knees, and it's my favorite blend of sexy and classy. My makeup is just like Mom taught me—natural but smooth—and I've pinned my hair halfway up with the rest curled around my shoulders. Leaning forward, I pop open my trusty tube of Red Revival lipstick and apply it to my lips.

This is all for my benefit, to make myself feel cute for the first time in forever. But I'd be absolutely lying to myself if I didn't admit a part of me hopes Ryan finds me attractive tonight.

That he sees my lips as a siren he has no wish to refuse.

"Stop it. Bad Kennedy," I point and hiss at myself (because yeah, I'm still that weirdo) and then hurry into the living room, where the girls are waiting. Ava's sitting on the edge of the couch and looks up from her phone. She's adorable in a blue dress and sheer sweater wrap that would be perfect for a school dance, and when she smiles at me, it's a shot to my heart.

Ever the most enthusiastic of the bunch, Mila hops up and rushes toward me. "Miss Kenny! You look so gorge-ful. That's gorgeous and beautiful put together."

Laughing, I grab her hands and twirl her. Her skirt flares out like a bell. "Why, thank you. You look prettific—that's pretty and terrific put together."

"Ooo, I like that!" She looks around me. "Uncle Ryan, Miss Kenny says I'm prettific!" Then she starts chasing Finley around the room.

I inhale a breath before turning toward Ryan—and promptly have to clutch the strap of my purse. Hard.

Because my hands want nothing more than to grab Ryan's lapels and pull him in for a hug.

Or, fine, much more than that.

He's wearing a crisp white dress shirt under a black dinner blazer and a pair of slim-fit dress pants that look tailor-made for him. His hair is gelled, the curls tamed, and a watch glints off his wrist, completing his look as Mr. Debonair. If Dr. Ryan Rosche was on *The Bachelor*, all the ladies would thank their lucky stars.

But other than the two young girls here with me, I don't have to compete tonight for this man's attention. Not if the look in his eyes means anything close to the vibe I'm sure my gaze is unintentionally giving off. "You look, um." I brush the side of my lips to make sure there's no drool present.

As if he can read my mind, Ryan's eyes laugh at me. "Dapsome?"

"Huh?"

He takes a step toward me and lowers his voice. "Dapper and handsome put together?" With a snort, I push at his arm and he laughs before spinning away toward the girls. "Excuse me, I'm looking for my nieces, Mila and Ava. Have you seen them?"

Mila stops chasing Finley around the room. "Uncle Ryan, silly. It's us."

He leans back, crosses his arm, strokes his non-existent beard. "No, that can't be true. You're little princesses."

Ava rolls her eyes, but a tiny smirk graces her lips. Then she stands and brushes out the creases in her dress. "Can we go? I'm starving."

Ryan waltzes to the front door and opens it, gesturing through it and bending at the waist. "After you, ladies."

The girls fly through and I start to follow, stopping just beside the door to grab my coat from the rack.

"Mila's right, you know."

I freeze, glance up at Ryan, who is right next to me—his breath warm on my bare shoulder. "About what?"

He gently takes my coat from me and helps me slip it on. "You've always been the most gorge-ful woman I've ever seen. But that dress …" His throat bobs and he fiddles with his collar. "Wow."

Is it strange that I take more pleasure from his incomplete thoughts than I ever did at Brooks's silver-tongued compliments? Maybe not. Those came with strings attached. Things expected.

But Ryan? He's just speaking what is clearly in his heart. And I know he means it, because his eyes are warm. Not filled with lust, but appreciation. Once again, he's seeing me for me—like no man ever has. If only he was anyone else.

Anyone but my boss.

"Thank you." The words are soft, full of all the feelings I can't say out loud. "And you do indeed look dapsome."

Before he can respond, I'm out the door and into the passenger seat of Ryan's truck. The evening weather has grown warmer this week, and given my clothing choice, I'm thankful for that. At the girls' request, Ryan cranks up Shania Twain and we all sing loudly—and off-key— the whole way to dinner.

And I realize something in those few moments.

This is the most at home I've felt since I moved back to San Diego. The happiest, too. The most settled. In these moments, I know what my purpose is. I know where I belong.

But what happens when the girls go back to their mom? What happens when this temporary gig … ends? What will I do then?

I guess that's a problem for another night, though. Tonight, it's my birthday—and I'm happy and free.

I've never been so full.

Or so satisfied.

"I think my stomach doubled in size." Placing my hands on my tummy, I puff it out and waddle down the restaurant steps like I'm pregnant. This makes Mila laugh and Ava roll her eyes in that affectionate near-teenage way she has. I'm taking it for affection, anyway.

"Mine too." Mila mimics me, and we walk arm and arm toward the parking lot.

"Hold up," Ryan calls from behind us. He shoves his hands into his pockets and looks around. It may be a Tuesday night, but Balboa Park is bustling with people, as is the restaurant where we just had the most delicious three-course dinner topped off with a coffee crème brûlée (the girls chose strawberry shortcake, but no way was I skipping coffee anything!). "You guys want to walk around a bit? I could use the exercise."

It's only a little after seven o'clock, still an hour before the girls' bedtime. And besides, it's a holiday—and my birthday. I'm not quite ready for it to end. "I'm game if you girls are."

Ava shrugs and Mila nods furiously before grabbing her sister's hand and tugging her forward. "Let's go see the lily pond! That's mama's favorite."

Ryan and I follow behind at a leisurely pace. The lush vegetation lines the sidewalks, and light music plays from the restaurant's outdoor speakers—something soft and romantic.

"Thanks for that lovely meal," I say after a few moments of silence. "I don't know how you scored that beautiful table by the window, but I'm grateful. Last-minute cancelation?"

He's watching his nieces as they stop to smell a few flowers next to a stone bench. "I know the owner."

"Really? How?"

A quick glance my way, a shrug, and his hands seem to move deeper into his pockets. "From work."

"Fellow doctor?"

He shakes his head.

Ah. He or someone he knows must have been a patient, and Ryan can't tell me anything else. I'm no doctor, but even I know about HIPAA laws.

We keep walking, and I can't help but notice how strong his profile looks against the cut of the moonlight streaming down around us. It's literally the perfect night—not too hot, not too cold. Clear skies.

Gorgeous man beside me.

Enough, Kennedy.

I clear my throat. "So you saved his life, then?"

"What?" Ryan halts, turns. "How did you—"

"No, no, don't confirm it. I don't want you getting in trouble." With a teasing smile, I poke him in the ribs before my better judgment can kick in. Then I start walking again, him following close behind. The girls are near the lily pond reflecting pool, and somehow, I feel pure peace rising from the surface. "It must feel pretty amazing. To save lives. To be so good at something."

"I'm not always good at it."

There's something dark and wounded in his words. Something that requires deeper examination. But I don't want to force it out of him. Still, he should know I'm here if he wants to talk about it. So, with Ava snapping pictures of the backlit Botanical Building—its large central dome lit up gold and beautiful, flanked by two identical long domed greenhouses—and Mila racing around the pond strewn with lily pads, I sit on a bench and pat the spot beside me.

Ryan takes the offering and sits too, leaning forward with his elbows on his knees. His pants hike up a bit, revealing black dress socks with white stethoscopes on them. I look away, suppressing a grin at the surprise clothing choice. Maybe his nieces bought them for him. Whoever did, it's adorable he's wearing them.

When he blows out a gloomy breath, my brain shifts back to the heaviness I can visibly see on his shoulders. But he doesn't say anything more. Maybe he truly can't. Or maybe he's not ready.

That's okay. I understand the sentiment.

Still, I want him to know that I'm a safe place. I'm not sure he has anyone else. From what I've seen, he's got his nieces and his sister … and his work. Surely he has work buddies, but in the three weeks that I've really known him, he's never taken the time to hang out with anyone else. Even before I became the nanny, I never saw anyone but Sophie and the girls come over to visit him.

I fiddle with the zipper on my jacket. "Nobody is good at their job all the time, but at least you know what you want to do with your life."

"I thought you wanted to go back to school."

"I do."

"But you don't know what you want to study?"

"The plan is marketing." I tug the zipper up, then down. Shake my head. "I don't know, though. Just the idea of business classes like economics and accounting makes me shudder. But marketing would be a good fit in terms of my skills. It's what I know from my life as an influencer, anyway."

Ryan sits up, slings his arm across the back of the bench, pivoting his body slightly toward me. "You don't have any desire to go back to that? I've heard you can make a good living off of it, and I'm sure you were good at it."

"I mean, I could. Except I'd be starting from scratch. My ex … well, he kind of defamed me after our breakup. While I did enjoy it, the whole thing was more his idea than mine." I chuckle, but it sounds more stran-gled than I mean for it to. "Told me I couldn't be so pretty for nothing. That I should use the assets I had, and that my best asset was my face." I grimace at how bitter I sound. Oops. Didn't mean for this to turn into a confessional.

"Geez, Kennedy. That guy …" His jaw clenches. "There's a lot more to you than your beauty. I hope you understand that."

Gaaaaah. I pull my coat tighter around myself, locking my hands underneath my armpits. "I do."

"Do you?"

"I'm trying to. My whole life, my mom kind of beat into me the idea of using beauty to my advantage. That's what she did, how she attracted all the men she did. But boyfriend after boyfriend would eventually fail her. They'd cheat on her, or they'd get busy with work and not pay enough attention to her, or the things they started out loving about her became the things that eventually annoyed them."

And okaaaay, yeah. Too much. Ryan does not need to know how screwed up my family was. Is.

I rush on. "But yeah. I guess when I think about my time as an influencer, my mind is split. I had a clear purpose—gain more followers, more collabs, more part-nerships—but in looking back, I'm not sure I ever really felt like me. Maybe if I did it again, without Brooks … but I don't know. I hated feeling like I had to be perfect in order to have an influence, you know? Because I'm the furthest thing from perfect, and all I ever felt like was a big fraud."

"I can definitely see the value in wanting to do some-thing where you feel like yourself. Where you feel authentic. I think a lot of us feel like frauds in this life, though. Every time I step into the hospital, I wonder if that's the day someone will discover that I'm not worthy of the faith that so many sick people are placing in me."

Oh, this man. "That's a lot of pressure."

"It can be."

"But you're making a difference. Saving lives."

"I can't always save them, Ken." And his voice sounds so forlorn, so broken. Maybe this is what he hates about his job—his inability to do it perfectly.

"No doctor can save everyone, Ryan. But you're still saving the ones you can." I purse my lips together. "I don't think there's a single thing I've ever posted that made a lick of difference in someone's actual life. It's a strange thing—thinking that just because someone follows you on social media, you're significant to them somehow. And then realizing, when it goes away, that you were never important to anyone at all." There's a burning in my chest as I say it, and oh, I've never wanted to escape a feeling more.

But Ryan lets me sit with it.

Better yet, he sits *with* me.

And I sit with him in his pain as well. We're sharing it, and suddenly, it doesn't feel quite so heavy.

Then, he speaks. "Kennedy, you don't have to have thousands of followers to be truly significant. To influence lives. You just need to make a difference in one life. And here, with us, you've made a difference in three." Ryan reaches across the bench for my knee, but blinks and pulls back again. Instead, he points at his nieces.

"Those girls right there wouldn't be thriving like they are without your influence."

All right, I'm officially going to cry. Oh, how I want to open my heart to this sweet man, at least tell him how much he and the girls have already influenced *my* life for the better. If I do, though, I'll fall even farther into serious *like* with him than I already am. I can feel myself teetering on the edge. It wouldn't take much for me to plummet. "Ryan—"

Thank goodness Mila chooses that moment to shout at us, and we stand to follow her and Ava as they continue our walk. We wind down paths overgrown with all kinds of plants—bushes and ferns, orchids and palm trees—and the fragrant scent of the coming spring fills my senses. Then we come upon one of my favorite spots in the park, where a larger-than-life fig tree that's over a century old spreads its branches wide and welcoming. It's ringed and protected by an iron waist-level fence and viewing steps.

The girls rush that way, but veer to the left. Seconds later, they're shouting a greeting at a beautiful brunette woman with two boys around the girls' age. The woman talks to the girls for a few moments before looking up and waving at Ryan. We approach and she meets us just in front of the entrance to the fig tree viewing. Ryan seems to know her—at least I hope he does, with the way he leans in for a hug.

My stupid heart bangs against my chest in protest.

"Hey, Marilyn." He pulls back. "How are you guys?"

"We're good. It's so wonderful to see you." She looks me up and down, but there's no malice or jealousy in her gaze. "Hi there. I'm Marilyn Goodrich, a friend of Sophie's. Our kids have known each other forever."

Oh. Now I feel kind of bad about my heart's subconscious reaction. "I'm Kennedy, the girls' nanny."

Eyebrows raised, Marilyn purses her lips in amusement as she looks me up and down. "Mmm." When she turns back to Ryan, she seems to put aside her thoughts about me because she frowns and squeezes his shoulder. "How's Soph doing?"

He glances at the girls, but they're more than occupied. Ava kicks at a rock as she talks shyly to the teenage boy, while Mila engages the other kid in a game of tag around the grass. "I talked with her last weekend. She's hanging in there. Getting clean. Again. Determined to do better. Again."

"Well"—another arm squeeze—"I'll keep praying that this time, it sticks."

"Thank you. She could use all the prayers she can get. We all could."

"I can't even imagine how hard this must be for you." She glances back at the girls, then down at her watch. "I know it's a school night, but would you be okay if I took the girls to get some ice cream at this little place around the corner? My boys have been dying to see them. I can bring them home by nine."

Ryan opens his mouth, probably to protest, but then looks over at me. "We could come too?"

I nod. "Sure." Despite the crème brûlée, I never turn down ice cream.

"Nonsense. You two enjoy some time off. Between the two of you, it sounds like you never get a break."

Marilyn pats his arm again. "You're a good man, Ryan Rosche. Take some time for yourself."

He hesitates. "If you're sure."

"I am. I've got an extra booster seat in my van, so we've got everything we need." She winks. "Enjoy the rest of your night." Sophie's friend turns to gather the children. They walk off—and then this part of the park is deserted.

Except for us.

Ryan grunts and walks up the steps to the tree observation deck. He starts reading the plaque dedicated to facts about the Moreton Fig Tree. Is he uncomfortable being alone with me? Or maybe he's just thinking about Sophie. We haven't talked much about her. Could be that's what he really needs to get off his chest.

And however un-smart it may be, I can't keep my distance from him anymore. Approaching, I hook my arm through his. The warmth of him penetrates my jacket and finds a home against my skin. "She's right, you know. You *are* a good man. Not many men would change their whole life around to accommodate two young girls like you have."

"They're family. Family—protecting those you love —is all that really matters."

"I totally agree." Because I'd do anything for Alexis, for Chloe. Even for Alexis's friends, who have looped me into their circle. I'd also do anything for Ava and Mila.

And Ryan too.

Dang it. I'm in too deep.

"I know you, Kennedy. You give your entire self to

people." Alexis was right about me. And now, I can't go back. Can't tell my heart to unhook itself, to release its hold. Once it's decided to be loyal to someone, it takes deep betrayal to turn its back on them. Even then, it's not always smart enough to turn away when it should. But I can't really imagine Ryan ever giving me a reason to turn away from him.

He's a freaking heartbreak waiting to happen, this one.

Ryan sighs. "Those girls have had so much of their lives stolen. I know what it's like, and I want to give them more than that. But I'm just their bachelor uncle who works a lot of hours. I feel so … inadequate."

"Are you a bachelor with a demanding career? Sure. But one who loves them more than anything. And that's not nothing, Ryan."

His gaze shifts to meet mine, and in that moment, I'm frozen. Crystalized. Shivering—and not just because of the breeze suddenly blowing the hair at the nape of my neck. It's the way his eyes study mine, the way his chin dips down, the way his body seems a magnet for my own.

The way his arm unhooks from mine and slides around my shoulders, tugging me closer to his body. "Thanks, Ken." His voice rumbles against my ear, which is pressed to the side of his chest. "But I wouldn't be able to do it without you. Normally that bothers me."

A few dead leaves blow from the huge tree, sweeping across my toes. "What? Asking for help?"

"Yeah."

"Why is that?"

"Since my parents died, it's just been Sophie and me. She took care of me—I was eleven, and she was barely an adult at eighteen—but the stress of it …" He sucks in a sharp breath, as if the thought is literally slicing through his lungs, making it hard to take in air. "She started drinking. All the time."

Oh, Ryan. "People often turn to things that aren't good for them when they're in pain." I slip my arm around his back, anchoring my hold on him as much as his is on me.

"I know you've been through a lot too. Must be why you seem so mature for your age."

I pull back so I can see him, then lift an eyebrow and cock my head in a teasing manner. "I'm twenty-four as of today. Not exactly a child."

"No, but …"

"But not ancient like you, Old Man?" I squeeze his side. (Which, side note, is kind of difficult to do given the hard planes of muscles there. But I digress.)

He chuckles. "Something like that, Young'un." Ryan looks at me out of the corner of his eye. "Is this what you imagined for your life? Being saddled with an old man for a boss, being a nanny? You have so much to offer the world. And I know we're more than halfway through the probation period …"

"First of all, you're not really *that* old."

"The stress of life tends to weigh a person down, age them, you know?" He slants his brow toward me. "Though it's easier with you here. But I don't want you to feel stuck. If you decide that this nanny life isn't for you, I'll understand."

"I ..." Biting my lip, I look away. Because I really want to say that I'm staying, that he's stuck with me. But I haven't fully made my decision about sticking it out. Or maybe just being here, like this, snuggled up against him, means I have. Ugh, I don't know. "It may not be what I imagined, Ryan, but it's better. A wonderful surprise. You and the girls have given me a sense of belonging and purpose I haven't had in a long time." If ever.

Ryan's arm tightens around me, and even through the fabric of my coat, I can feel his thumb stroking my shoulder. And oh, how I want to turn into his arms, fully embrace him, give him all of me.

But I don't want to change our dynamic, either. I'm ... scared. Scared that we'll fall for each other, scared that things will go south, scared that I'll then be forced to find a new job—to find a new home. That I'll be separated from those girls who have come to mean so much to me already.

I'm scared to become my mother, always chasing a home. Never finding it.

We've both been quiet for a while, and finally, Ryan says, "I just realized that I kind of sprung this outing on you. You probably had friends you wanted to hang out with."

I snort. "Hmm, let's see. Alexis is visiting Dax for a few days, and Chloe's parents asked her to attend some charity thing. All of my other friends are married or engaged, and this is Valentine's Day. So actually, Mila was telling the truth. I'd planned to watch TV."

"The Bachelor?" His eyes twinkle against the dark sky.

"Maaaaaybe."

"You were going to watch it without me?"

I fake a wince. "I may have already watched a few episodes while you were working overnights this week."

"How could you?" He clutches his chest. "I wanted to know what happens next."

I laugh. "Right."

"This must be remedied. Let's go catch an episode before the girls get home. Maybe another few after I get them to bed. You can fill me in on what I missed."

It sounds divine—but is it a good idea? *You know it's not, Kennedy.* "Won't that be too late for you? I know you like to be in bed by ten, Old Man."

"Ha ha. For your information, I'm off tomorrow, and it would be a nice way to wind down."

"Wait, you're serious?" I slide gently out from under his arm and turn to face him fully. Instantly, I'm doused with cold and my body regrets the action. "You want to keep watching with me?"

"Sure, why not?" His favorite expression.

"And you don't find it immature of me to watch stuff like that?" The words were supposed to be teasing, but there's a real question there. I mean, Ryan *is* eleven years older than me (well, ten and some months, but who's counting?). Brooks was only twenty-six, and *he* called my shows dumb more times than I can count.

But Ryan just cups my elbow gently in one of his

large hands. It takes all my willpower not to melt into his touch. Nah, too late. *Splat.* I'm a puddle at his feet.

"Kennedy, watching *The Bachelor* with you is the most fun I've had in a long time. I like that you don't take everything so seriously. I … I need that in my life. Someone to remind me to have fun." He cocks his head. "But if you have somewhere else to be or something else to do, I don't want to keep you."

I duck my head and smile, because WHAT ELSE AM I SUPPOSED TO DO WITH THAT RESPONSE? "No, there's nowhere else I have to be. And …"

Don't say it, don't say it …

Ugh, who am I kidding? I *have* to say it. The words are threatening to burst right out of my chest if I don't.

I fiddle with my necklace, gathering the courage to look back up at him. When I do, the moonlight reflects off his irises. "There's nowhere else I'd rather be, either."

Which is—unfortunately for me—the absolute truth.

"Good," is his soft reply. "Same here."

eleven

· · ·

THERE'S JUST something about the beach in the wintertime. It's more muted, somehow, maybe because of the cold. Windier too. But it's no less wonderful.

Even if I got here by doing the one thing I abhor above all others.

"I still can't believe you made me run that whole way." I am doubled over, gloved hands on my knees, and my rib cage feels like it might burst from the exertion.

"I don't think anyone can *make* you do anything." Ryan's next to me in his jogging pants, beanie, and a sweat-slicking shirt. Today, he's Finley-less. Apparently, the dog has been known to go nuts when he sees the gulls, and Ryan didn't feel like dealing with that today.

"No, but you were highly convincing, luring me out of bed this morning with that espresso." After a late night of reality TV—and lots of laughter—it felt impossible to get up this morning, but since Ryan was off, he got the girls to school. Then he came home with a chocolate croissant and a coffee from Java Awakening, knocked on my door, and asked if I'd like to join him on his run. "My brain was still muddled when I agreed to it. You're not allowed to ask me things before I've had coffee."

It's mid-morning and we're on the boardwalk that's streaked with sand. Thankfully the breeze off the ocean has calmed down, because for the first mile of our run, I thought my face was going to permanently freeze in a grimace. Once I settled into the run, though, I kind of enjoyed myself. Not the screaming of my thigh muscles or the catch in my side or the angry wind in my face—duh. But running alongside Ryan, who was clearly going more slowly so I could keep pace with him, who looks so confident and in his element, who kept encouraging me when I thought I couldn't go another step?

Yeah. That was all pretty great.

"I'll remember that next time." He laughs and points to a coffee and cocoa cart next to a patch of grass just off the boardwalk. "Want to take a rest before we head back?"

My body protests the idea of running another step, much less the three miles back to his truck. I know he'd totally go back and get it himself and drive over to pick me up, but the whole reason I said yes was because I didn't want our time together to end. And that hasn't stopped just because I'm now well-caffeinated.

It also doesn't stop me from wanting even more caffeine, maybe this time in the form of hot chocolate. "Um, yes, please."

We each grab a cocoa and then walk toward the long pier that juts out in the sea. Given it's the middle of the week, and the middle of the morning, there aren't many people out here on the uneven planks of wood. The breeze picks up again, maybe because we're out on the water, but it's too beautiful not to be drawn out there. Like many days in San Diego, clouds cover the sky, but bits of light peek through too—a reminder of something, a deeper truth that's just niggling at my conscious.

As we move closer to the end of the pier, my fingers draw warmth from my cup and I bring it closer to my face, the steam and scent of chocolate hitting my lips and nose. Then I take a sip and the rich liquid feels like velvet going down. A hint of melted marshmallow clings to my lips. "That's the best cocoa I've ever had."

Ryan stops at the railing and turns, smiling at me. "I'm glad you're enjoying it." His eyes roam my face before stopping on my mouth.

My fingers flex against the cardboard cup in my hand.

"You've got something ..." He points to his upper lip.

Oops. Lifting a hand, I start to reach for the spot on my own lip, but remember I'm wearing gloves and don't want them to get dirty. I begin to tug one off, but Ryan snaps his off in two seconds and takes a step toward me. My heart is threatening anarchy as Ryan delicately smooths his thumb across the corner of my upper lip.

It takes everything in me not to kiss that thumb before it moves away.

Does he hear my involuntary sigh? Maybe we're on dangerous ground here, but at the moment, I can't be bothered to care. And maybe he doesn't either, because he eases closer, his eyes searching mine for something—permission, perhaps? And I find myself unable to refuse him anything right now.

With the utmost care, his hand returns to me, finding a stray piece of hair that's come loose from my beanie. Like the hair is a precious golden thread woven by Rumpelstiltskin himself, Ryan's thumb and forefinger stroke the top half of it before gently tucking it back into my hat. Then his thumb continues its descent down the side of my face, hopping over to the shell of my ear under the beanie, before popping back out and skimming my jaw.

How is it possible that this light, gentle touch is more powerful than all the ways Brooks—or any other boyfriend—ever touched me? But there's an awe in Ryan's eyes that I never saw on any of *their* faces.

And I know that he is absolutely going to kiss me in this moment.

And I'm absolutely going to let him.

My eyes flutter closed and I can feel the warm tingle of his breath on my lips before—

"Ryan?"

I jerk away at the feminine voice, my eyes flying back open.

Ryan's looking behind me, his face whiter than I've ever seen it. "Jillian?"

Turning, I find a very pregnant woman who looks about my age walking in our direction. She's beautiful with her auburn hair pulled back, her pale skin, and bright blue eyes that shimmer as she takes in the length of Ryan. When she gets to the railing—huffing and puffing—she leans against it like she needs the support. But the whole time, her eyes never leave Ryan. "Ryan Rosche." She's got the same accent as Ryan's, but it's sharper, more prominent.

Dare I say, grating? But maybe that's just because she's drinking him in like she's dying of thirst in a desert and he's her oasis.

"What are you doing here?" he asks. "I thought you moved to L.A."

She swipes the air, and Ryan would have to be blind not to see the rock on her hand. "We moved back six months ago when we found out about this little number." Laughing, she points to her stomach, but I can hear something strained in her giggle. It's too high-pitched, too tight. Too much. Like she's only pretending to be happy.

Or maybe I'm reading way too much into it.

Ryan's still blinking at her, running his hand along his jaw. "We?"

"Oh, me and my husband Douglas. He's a director in LA, but we both have family here. And you know, family is the most important thing."

"Uh huh," he finally says. "Well, that's … something."

I nearly snort, but this doesn't seem to be a snorting matter. Not if what I see in his eyes truly is pain like I suspect.

The silence hangs between them—us all—like a

heavy blanket that's been doused with water over and over again, never given a chance to dry. Then Jillian speaks. "I just couldn't believe my eyes when I saw you there. You look so … healthy."

Healthy? What's that supposed to mean?

There's a ragged intake of air from Ryan and he turns his head to look down at the water where it's lapping against the legs of the pier. I want so badly to offer him my support, but don't know what I could say.

Maybe I don't need to say anything, though.

So I slide my hand into his and squeeze. His gaze shifts to me, surprise there, then softening. His shoulders straighten and he nods, as if resolving something in his mind. "Thanks, Jillian. I've been in remission for three years now."

Remission? From what?

Jillian tucks a piece of hair behind her ear, cocking her head. "I'm so happy for you." She looks at our joined hands, and smiles tightly and decidedly *not* happily. "For both of you."

"Oh—" he starts to protest.

"Thank you," I interrupt and lean my head against his shoulder. Because no way is this woman who is so obviously Ryan's ex (and would quite possibly like to become his *ex* ex despite the ring on her finger) getting her claws back into him.

He threads our fingers together and squeezes my hand this time. "Yes, thank you. It was good to see you, Jillian. I wish you and Douglas all good things."

She bites her lip, looking like she wants to say more,

but finally just nods. "Same to you, Ryan. And ..." She finally meets my gaze.

"Kennedy."

"Kennedy." She swallows. "That's real pretty."

Okay, maybe there's something genuine about her. Maybe she just got a little lost somewhere along the way. But she hurt Ryan somehow, and that's hard to forgive.

"Bye," Jillian whispers before turning and waddling away. She nearly trips on a board that's a bit higher than the one behind it.

Dropping my hand, Ryan steps forward to help, but then Jillian steadies herself and walks away, head held high.

"You okay?"

His jaw tense, he faces the railing again. "That was ... we used to be together."

I turn so we're shoulder to shoulder, leaning forward against the wooden beam. "I gathered."

"Told you. You're perceptive."

The haze of the morning is beginning to burn off the water, making things clearer. So clear that my heart skips when I see movement out a ways. Dolphins. There's a whole pod of them, kicking and jumping, some just skimming the water before going below again. The sight is worth all the muscle ache it took to get here.

"It didn't take much perception to see that she misses you and wishes she had you back."

He shakes his head. "That can't be true. She's the one who dumped me."

Hmm. "So. What's this about remission?"

He's quiet, lips pursed. Is he going to tell me what happened or change the subject? But either way, I don't want him to feel trapped. He doesn't *have* to tell me anything, even if I'm dying to know.

I nudge him with my elbow and move my head back toward the beach. We start walking and, after exiting the pier, toss our half-empty and now-cold cups of cocoa into the nearest trash can. Before we can begin our trek down the boardwalk in the direction of Ryan's truck, he stops and inclines his head toward the sand. "Want to?"

"Sure, why not?"

A tiny smile flickers across his lips as he catches my mimicking of him. We remove our shoes and hold them while we walk down the sand, far enough in so the waves don't lick our ankles, but close enough that our feet smoosh into the damp sand. Ryan hasn't taken up my hand again, and I don't know if I want him to.

Well, I want him to.

Obviously.

I just don't know if we should. I don't know yet if this is a good idea. Of course, if I thought spending time alone with him was going to bring me any clarity on the matter, then that was a mega mistake. Clearly I can't think straight around the man.

We've been walking for a while—a slow, chilling amble—when he finally continues our conversation. "I had cancer. Hodgkin's lymphoma. About three and a half years ago."

Oh, wow. "That must have been rough."

"Not gonna lie, it was a hard time. Especially ..." He tugs his beanie down farther over the tops of his ears.

"Jillian and I were pretty serious. She worked the front desk at the hospital, but that was never her dream. Her dream was to make it as an actress. I knew when we started dating that she wanted to move to LA someday, and I was supportive, though I made it clear that I could never move away from my sister and nieces. I mean, I moved here in the first place when Ava was born because Sophie's ex couldn't be counted on to help out. And then when Jillian and I were together, things were even worse for Sophie."

"And you were probably over there all the time helping out."

He shrugs, which I take as a yes. "Mila was just a baby. Sophie was trying to stay clean for the girls' sake, but the girls' dad had just left and she was struggling big time. But Jillian understood. She said taking care of those you love is the biggest privilege." Ryan huffs. "But when I got diagnosed, she stuck it out for exactly one chemo session before she decided it was time for her to move to LA."

"Wait, what? How long had you been dating?"

"We were engaged, Kennedy."

I don't expect the gut punch, but when it comes, I can barely breathe. "I'm so sorry, Ryan."

"I knew better than to propose to her. It was a mistake. But I was in love, you know? I found someone who supported me in my career, understood the demanding hours, accepted my commitment to my family."

Sailboats pass one another in the distance, stately voyagers across the horizon. A sadness I can't explain twists and roils in my gut. "That doesn't sound like a mistake to me."

"I let my dream—to have a family of my own—overshadow hers. Basically, I asked her to give hers up."

"It sounds to me like she agreed to marry you."

"Yeah, but …"

"But what? She was a grown woman, wasn't she? She made her own decision."

He glances at me out of the corner of his eye. Frowns. "She was only twenty-three at the time. She had her whole life ahead of her, all her dreams just waiting for her."

I blink, then recall his reaction to finding out my age. Is that why he said what he did last night? *"Is this what you imagined for your life? Being saddled with an old man for a boss?"*

Doesn't he know that I'm not Jillian?

The sorrow in his eyes is too much. Dropping my shoes, I step forward and hug him around the waist. And when his own shoes hit the sand and Ryan wraps me up in his strong arms, I snuggle down deep into his hold. "So who took care of you when you were sick?" Because chemo is no joke. My mom went through it for a few months before she decided it was no way to live, quit, and died shortly thereafter. I well remember the nausea, days spent next to the toilet, providing cool cloths for her head, cleaning up her messes, helping her back to bed before heading right back to the bathroom. The sores in her mouth. The hair loss. The fatigue.

Nobody should go through that alone.

"No one."

What? "What about Sophie?"

"I told you. She was busy with the girls, trying to keep her life on track. I couldn't ask her to also worry about taking care of me." His hand moves up and down my spine, like he's the one comforting me instead of vice versa. "I survived. It was no big deal."

I pull back and stare up at him. "Ryan, I'm sorry, but that's a very big deal. You're always taking care of everyone else. You deserve to have someone take care of you every now and then too."

"I'm happy to be the caretaker. My dad always said, 'Spending your life taking care of others is the most worthwhile calling.'"

Something clicks. "Is that why you became a doctor?"

He nods. "Dad was a doctor too, actually." His nose is red from the cold—I can hardly feel my own, so it's just an assumption—but there's only warmth here in his arms. "And"—his voice breaks—"just before he died at the hospital, after the car accident, he grabbed my hand and told me to take care of my sister, even though she was older. I dunno. Maybe he told her the same thing about me. Either way, I promised him I would." His body shudders, like he's trying to hold in the tears.

"And you've done well by that promise."

"It doesn't feel like it. Look at where she is now."

"She is in jail because of her own choices." My hands leave his back and drift to his face. I cup his cheeks in my palms and angle his head down so he can't miss what I'm saying. "You can't control her actions any more than you could control Jillian's."

"I know that logically. But I still feel like a failure."

"Old Man Dr. Ryan Rosche"—he chuckles at that—"you are *anything* but a failure. And anyone who says otherwise can answer to me."

"Oh, yeah?" He moves his face down, down, until our noses are touching.

Oops. This moment got away from me.

But I have no desire to get away from it.

"Yeah," I whisper before lifting up on my tiptoes and fusing my lips to his. It only takes a second for him to respond, to tug me closer, to move his hands up the length of my back and into my hair. The action sends my hat flying to the ground, but I don't care in the slightest. Not when his mouth does what I've been dying for it to do for months, since the first time I spoke to him on my sister's porch.

He tastes like chocolate and all good things, like the salted ocean in the air, and every one of my senses is engaged as my hands slide from his face and loop around the back of his neck. My bare toes curl into the sand, but that does nothing to anchor me. I feel like I could be swept out to sea at any moment.

Never in my life has anyone kissed me like Ryan Rosche is kissing me—and that thought takes me out of this present moment, to the past.

To my mistakes.

To the whole reason I was going to avoid this particular scenario in the first place.

I pull back rather suddenly, opening my eyes.

Ryan does the same and blinks against the light. "Kennedy?"

"I ... I'm sorry. We were supposed to keep things professional."

"We were." Still, he doesn't loosen his hold. "But things have clearly evolved."

"Should they, though?"

"Only if you want them to." Then I'm back pressed against his chest, hugging him like he's my life preserver in the storm. His heartbeat pounds against his chest, against my ear, in time with my own fears. "Do you?"

"I just ... I don't know." A tear falls down my cheek, because I can see that this is hurting him. But better for us to be hurt a little now instead of a lot later. Right? "I'm sorry. I like you, I do. It's just ... there's a lot you don't know about me." *A lot you'd probably run from if you did.* "I'm a mess."

"Kennedy, we're all messes." His lips press a gentle kiss against my forehead. "But I don't want to cross any lines you're not sure about. I'm sorry if I got carried away."

"Clearly I did too." I close my eyes. "Can I just have some time to think about this? And you should too."

"I already know what I want."

Gah. There's nothing I want to shout more than *I surrender!* But Mom always leaped before she looked, and I can't forget what that got her.

"But"—his hands squeeze my waist as he pulls back to look at me again—"I want you to be sure too. So, please. Take all the time you need. I'm not going anywhere."

twelve

. . .

IN THIS MOMENT, I've never been more thankful for girlfriends and karaoke.

Because instead of obsessing about what happened earlier this week—which, let's face it, I've done the entirety of the last two and a half days since Ryan and I ran back to his truck after our kiss—I can think about my friends' drama.

"This wedding is going to have lace coming out its ears." Lauren practically shouts at us across a large circular booth inside a karaoke bar that Kayla claims is "as amazing as the moment when Luke blows up the Death Star." Given the wooden tables splattered with sticky residue, the overpriced drinks, and the disco ball overhead, I'm thinking she oversold it.

But none of that matters. All of us girls are here for a rare night together, and I am here for it.

"Lace is pretty," Evie says as she sips on her mudslide. (When questioned about whether nursing moms could drink alcohol, Kayla informed us all about the phenomenon known as pumping and dumping. Will wonders never cease?)

"Yeah." From her spot sitting beside Evie, Shelby nods so hard she looks like a bobblehead. "I'm sure every royal wedding has at least some lace, right? Your coordinator must know what she's doing."

Holding her cosmo in one hand, Kayla taps Evie's shoulder with the other. "But the point is, Lauren haaaaates lace." She's standing-slash-dancing in the only spot at the table that doesn't have a booth attached. Behind her, two college-aged guys are five thousand sheets to the wind and singing about friends in low places. One's not half bad, but the other is bringing him waaaay down. "And she shouldn't have lace if she doesn't want lace."

Seems to me Kayla maybe should eat some food, given she's only had half her drink and is already slurring her words. Or maybe she's just super tired. I heard Baby Rey was up five times last night.

The conversation continues and Chloe dives into a story about the time her parents hired "Felicia Flutterbum" to plan her sixteenth birthday party. Meanwhile, from my spot in the dead center of the booth (ah, no escape!), I pick up my fork and wave it at Alexis, who is sitting on the opposite end of the booth, Chloe and bodyguard Tia between us. Her bright green hair is in its usual braid, though she did comply with Kayla's request that we all get dressy ("because, ladies, my wardrobe these days consists of stretchy pants and nursing bras that unsnap and I need this!").

When I catch my sister's eye, she scrunches her nose at me. I point to the basket of chips in the middle of the table, then at Kayla, who has one arm above her head and is twirling in her bright red dress that honestly looks amazing considering she just gave birth a month or so ago.

Alexis's eyes widen and she grabs a few chips, shoving them into Kayla's hands and saying something I can't hear.

Kayla rolls her eyes but eats the chips.

"And get this," Chloe continues with her story. "Instead of getting 'N Sync impersonators like I requested, she hired a Beatles band. No offense to those who love the yellow submarine, but—"

"But no one tops 'N Sync!" Lauren pounds her fist on the table.

"Exactly. I'm glad someone else understands my obsession."

"Wouldn't that be amazing at a wedding?" Lauren's chin sinks onto her propped-up hand and she smiles and sighs. "'N Sync impersonators?"

We all look at each other and laugh. Good-natured Lauren—future princess of Kentonia and eventual queen—sticks her tongue out at us and makes a funny face.

Kayla teeters on her four-inch heels, then grabs the table and steadies herself. "I think you have about as much chance of that happening as—"

"Please don't make a stupid *Star Wars* reference again." Alexis groans and drains her gin and tonic.

Throwing a hand on her hip, Kayla glares at Alexis.

"Oh, like you don't make dumb Marvel references all the time. Thor this, Captain America that. Please. Give me Luke and Han any day."

The two of them start bickering, while the rest of us shake our heads. Shelby, ever the peacemaker, bites her lip and points to the stage. "Does anyone want to join me?"

From what I've heard, there's no way she would have even considered singing karaoke in front of a crowd before her starring role last summer in the Cinderella musical at the school where she works. That was the same time that she became brave enough to finally tell Eric, her longtime best friend and now fiancé, how much she loves him.

And there's something about seeing her climb from the booth—hauling Kayla, Lauren, Chloe, and Tia along in her wake—that gives me hope. If she can change her life so drastically, then maybe, despite my past, there's hope for me.

I take a salty chip in hand and bite into it. The booth is a lot less crowded with just me, Alexis, and Evie left behind to cheer on our friends. They gather at the DJ booth to pick out a song and are soon standing on the stage, giggling and shoving the two microphones around until Kayla and Shelby both agree to hold them.

Sonny and Cher's "I Got You, Babe," starts playing—and the second I hear it, the tears start coming.

Alexis's arm is around me in a flash, and Evie looks at us with concern in her eyes. "What's wrong, Kennedy?"

I wave my hand a bit, trying to focus on my friends

—because yes, they *are* my friends, even if they were Alexis's first—as they sing and sway, their arms hooked around each other's backs. The crowd cheers for them, but they really only have eyes for each other.

Alexis answers for me. "This was her mom's favorite song."

"Oh." Evie's eyes tell me she understands. And I know she does. She lost someone too, a long time ago. "If she was anything like you, she must have been very special."

I grab a paper cocktail napkin and start ripping it into shreds. "Not if you ask my grandmother."

"Who cares what that old biddy thinks?" Alexis squeezes my shoulder, then hands me another napkin when mine is in tatters.

I take it from her and *rip, rip, rip.* "You didn't like my mom either."

"That's not true."

I lift my eyebrows at her.

"Did I think she could have made better decisions in the love department, and in prioritizing you and your needs? Yeah." Dropping her hand from my shoulders, Alexis stabs a straw into her glass of water and swirls it violently around. If I could hear anything but her words and Sonny and Cher's song being butchered by everyone but Shelby, I'd probably hear the ice clinking against the side of the cup. "But your grandma is too harsh. Pippa was many things, but she wasn't all bad. She was fun, and she did love you. I just think she didn't know how to show it all the time. And I think she got lost, you know? Having Martha for a mom couldn't have been a picnic. She never thinks anyone but her is good enough for the Montgomery name, and that's bound to screw with a person."

I arch an eyebrow. "You think?"

"I didn't mean you. You're a Matkin."

"That legacy isn't much better." A man with two families, each a secret from the other.

Evie watches us with sympathy in her gaze. Then she reaches across the table, laying a hand on my arm. "Whatever your family and your legacy, you're your own person, Kennedy. And from what I've seen in the short time I've known you, you are amazing. Loyal, kind, always anticipating the needs of others, forgiving. Empathy is your superpower. That's a rare gift."

Aaaaand there come the tears again.

Alexis shoves another napkin into my empty fingers. "She's right."

"Maybe." I sniffle and set this napkin down on the table, looking up into her eyes and channeling Shelby's bravery. "But all that *some* people can see are the mistakes I've made. The ways I don't measure up. The ways I'm just like my mother when it comes to men and my bad judgment."

At this, Alexis shifts sideways in her chair, blinking at me. "What? Do you mean … me?"

Oh, I didn't want to hurt her. But if I'm ever going to become truly mature, truly change, then I have to be a thousand percent honest with the people I love. "I know you love me, A, but you don't believe in me."

Her mouth falls open, and she squeaks out a protest.

Looking between us, Evie says, "Excuse me, I need

to use the restroom," before scooting out of the booth just as the other women's song is ending. Ugh. Maybe I should take advantage of the open booth and just go home. The last thing I want is to cause a scene. But I don't want to leave either. I'd just have to go back to the house I share with the girls … and Ryan.

Oh man. What am I going to do about Ryan? I'd forgotten about that for about two seconds. But maybe I need to work on *this* relationship with Alexis, this part of me and my past, before I can think about a future.

Alexis takes a few long moments to process what I've said. She fiddles with the straw, takes a drink, fiddles again, drinks again. Finally, she inhales deeply. "Kennedy, do you have any idea how stinking proud of you I am?"

"What? I thought …"

"I've been a terrible sister if I've given you the impression I don't believe in you. Stars, that's the *last* thing I want to communicate. I guess I'm just tough on you *because* I believe in you so much. I want you to reach your full potential."

"You told me that I'm the kind of woman who is easily swayed by handsome men." If she's challenging me, then I'm gonna challenge her right back. "That sounds an awful lot like not believing in me."

"Yeah, I did say that, didn't I?" She bites her lip. "I'm sorry, Ken. It was just so hard, you know? Seeing you with Brooks, someone who diminished your light, who didn't care what you wanted. He was so selfish, and you were so loyal that you just let him walk all over you."

"You're right. I was stupid." I sigh. "Just like Mom."

"I didn't mean that."

"Well, Gran sure did. Right after I talked with you, she lectured me on turning out just like my mother. All she can see when she looks at me is my mom's biggest mistake—falling for a con man who knocked her up, proposed to her even though he was already married, and then left her with a look-alike brat when he died."

Alexis winces at my description of our father—and myself—but I'm just repeating words I heard Gran say to my mom a long time ago. "That woman ... Ugh, Kennedy. I'm so sorry if my words sounded like anything she's ever said to you. I just love you so much. I want you to be happy."

Tilting my head, I smooth my thumb and forefinger down my dangling earring. "But you don't trust me enough to choose that happiness."

"I never meant to communicate that, and if I did, then I'm so sorry." Alexis pauses, frowning. "Ken, I'm your sister. Since I found out about you, I've wanted to protect you. But you're more than capable of making your own decisions. Of making *good* decisions."

I chew the inside of my cheek. "You really think so?"

"Of course, and the fact you didn't know I believed that is on me."

"I've just made so many mistakes. Blowing dad's inheritance money, getting kicked out of school, Brooks …"

Alexis grunts. "None of us, myself included, is the sum of our mistakes. It's what we do with our failures that matter, not the failures themselves."

"That's the problem. I don't *know* what to do. What if

… what if there's nothing I'm really good at? I think I want to go back to school, but is marketing what I really want to study? I'm afraid to even admit that, because I want to be the opposite of what I've been. I want to move from aimless to purpose-filled. But how can I when I don't fully know what it is I want?"

You know what you want, Kennedy. At least, you know WHO you want.

Alexis grabs my hand and tugs, like she always does when she's making a point and really wants me to listen. It's so bossy and big sister-y of her—and I love her for it. "Kennedy, I'm thirty-three years old and I just figured out a few months ago that not all men are pigs after all. Six months ago, my biggest dream was to pay off my house so I didn't have to find more roommates when all of my friends eventually moved out and got married. I was gonna be the crazy cat lady."

I sniff-chuckle at that.

"But"—she squeezes—"I'm still learning and growing and figuring out that what I want isn't tied to a place or a thing. It's tied to people. To you. To Dax. To those crazy women over there who are beginning to freak me out with the way they're staring at us."

I glance up to find her friends hovering at a nearby empty cocktail table, all of them watching us intently as if they're trying to read our lips. And that's all I need to start laughing so hard my stomach hurts. Then, I sober up quick. "What would I do without you, Sis?"

She squeezes my elbow. "Good thing you'll never have to find out."

Then we wave the women back over. And as the

chatter restarts, as the chaos swirls, the laughter picks up and is tossed back and forth with ease. I settle against the cushioned booth and wonder where I go from here. Is it possible that I *could* have Ryan? That I wouldn't be a complete idiot to risk my nanny job, to say no to Gran's offer?

That I could be just Kennedy? Not Pippa's daughter or Martha's granddaughter or the "illegitimate" offspring of Quincy Matkin?

I feel a shift somewhere deep inside myself. A shift toward … hope. And I recall Chloe's words from earlier this week. *"Maybe Dr. Ryan is your future—if you can just get past the fear of making another mistake and start trusting yourself again."*

Could she be right? How do I decide?

Just take a beat, Kennedy. You don't have to make any decisions tonight.

But despite that very rational thought, all I want to do is race home and tell Ryan—show him—exactly what that hope looks like in translation.

thirteen

TODAY IS THE DAY. I'm going to tell Ryan how I feel —what I want.

And about all the reasons why he might not want me back. I'm gonna lay it all out there for him. And if he still decides he wants to give this a go … well, then I'm all in.

Which is only mildly terrifying.

Rolling out of the warm bed, I press my toes into the carpet and try to remember to breathe. It took me a long time to fall asleep last night after returning home just past midnight (and several rounds of forced karaoke that were actually quite fun and freeing). Ryan was already in bed when I got back, which was not shocking, given his old man bedtime hours. But that meant I couldn't blurt out my feelings in a karaoke- and daiquiri-inspired confessional and instead lay in bed looking at my ceiling and imagining the perfect words I will say tonight after he gets home from work and the girls go to bed.

Bleary-eyed and yawning, I tug on my fluffy white robe over my pajamas and trudge out to make myself some coffee. Finley is lying outside of my room, and his tongue pops out as he raises his head. I pet him with my foot and then step over him into the hallway.

The house is quiet, a surprise given the eight o'clock hour and the fact it's Saturday—and everyone knows that kids only sleep in on the days they're not supposed to and are up at the crack of dawn on the weekend. I peek into Mila's room just to be sure she isn't playing quietly or reading, but no, she's tucked into her Disney princess-themed comforter Ryan brought home for her after Ava painted her room. Her steady breathing confirms she's asleep.

Sweet. A morning to myself even while I'm on duty. This is a rare treat, but I'm not complaining.

Finley's my shadow as I finish my trek down the hallway and out into the living room, then onto the kitchen where I find a note on the espresso machine in Ryan's masculine block lettering: *Got my shift today extended to twenty-four hours—someone's out sick. Shouldn't affect your schedule too much unless you had plans tonight. If that's the case, text me and I'll find a sitter.*

No! That means he won't be home until tomorrow, and he'll of course need to sleep since he rarely gets much shut-eye during those longer shifts. Plus I have to work at Java Awakening until closing tomorrow—so basically, I've got nearly two days of torturous thoughts and *what-ifs* ahead of me.

After I put some food in Finley's bowl, I start on my coffee while my brain buzzes. It's not as if I think he's changed his mind. He seemed pretty sure what he wanted on Wednesday during our run. But he hasn't said anything since then, and hasn't sought me out to spend time with me. I'm guessing he just doesn't want me to feel pressured.

But what if he *has* changed his mind?

Ugh, see? Torturous thoughts.

Chiding myself, I grab my favorite mug of Ryan's from the cabinet. It was made by a young Ava at one of those pottery places, painted bright purple and orange, with the painted colors mixed together on some of the edges, creating black splotches that would be unsightly if painted by an adult but are adorable when painted by a kid. But that's not the best part, which is what the mug says: "World's Best Hunkle." When I inquired about it, Ryan told me that's what he teasingly called himself when Ava was first born, and apparently she believed that was the correct word and spelling of "uncle" until she was eight.

I run my thumb along the smooth glazed surface. Only a man who is devoted to his nieces would keep and use a mug like this. But such is the man I'm starting to fall in love with.

Whoa there, Kennedy. Love?

I really need some caffeine. My brain just didn't come up with the right word.

Yes, it did, taunts my heart.

And I kind of think it's right. Oh my sheesh.

Can't think about this, can't think about this … I grab

my phone, text Ryan that I'm good to watch the girls tonight, and then make myself some avocado toast and coffee in the blessed silence. After I eat, I tidy up the living room, which has evidence of the movie night Ryan and Mila had last night while Ava hung out at a friend's house. (I know she was there because she texted me while I was at the bar, asking how to tell if a boy likes you. I texted back that that was a conversation I'd be happy to have in person, but that at her age it could look like anything from pulling her hair to trying to hold her hand since boys in junior high tend to be ignorant of social cues. She sent back a laughing emoji.)

Once everything is clean and smelling of the lemon furniture polish I used, I glance at the clock. Hmmm. Okay. Nine-thirty? Something's going on. Why aren't the girls up yet?

I head for Ava's room first, even though she actually does tend to sleep in on the weekends. When I peek in, I find her in bed scrolling her phone, shadows ringing the outside circle of her face. She glances up at me and I wave into the dark. "Good morning. Want some breakfast?"

She shakes her head. "I think I might be starting my period soon. My stomach hurts."

"Aw, I'm sorry to hear that. Girl problems are no joke. You want a heating pad? Meds? Anything?"

"I think I just wanna go back to sleep."

"Sure thing. Just text me if you need me and don't feel like getting up."

"Thanks, Kennedy." She blinks back at me, and I just want to rush to her and pull her into a huge hug.

Of course, I don't because I like that she's actually talking to me now. No sense in scaring her off and starting from scratch. "Anytime. Sweet dreams, girl."

I ease her door shut and peek in on Mila again. She's rolling over in her bed, moaning lightly. A flicker of alarm pulses through me and I step into her room. I don't need to turn on the lamp since the light from outside is coming through her window. Her eyes are shut, but the hair around her scalp looks damp, and when I lower myself onto her bed beside her and smooth back her bangs, the fever is obvious.

Should I wake her or let her sleep?

But the decision is made for me when she clutches her stomach and groans again. I stroke her hair and her eyes flutter open. "Mommy?"

Poor, sweet girl. I lean closer and press a kiss to her hot forehead. "Morning, sweetie. It's Kennedy."

"My tummy hurts." And Mila starts to cry. "I want my mommy."

Tears fill my own eyes, not only because I'm a sympathy crier, but because I fully understand the sentiment. As much as Pippa wasn't always the best mom, whenever I was sick, she was right there, holding me, watching TV with me, bringing me whatever I needed.

"I know, love. But I'm here right now."

Then Mila sits up suddenly, turns, and vomits all over my lap—and starts to cry harder.

Okay. Definitely not how I saw this day going.

I ease the crying sweetheart from her bed and carry her to the bathroom, where she vomits again into the toilet. When she finishes, I wash her clean with a cloth, get some fresh clothes for her, and bring her out to the couch, which I first cover with an old blanket. Then I grab an emesis basin from underneath the bathroom cabinets and deposit it beside her before turning on some Saturday morning cartoons.

"Don't leave me alone, Miss Kenny," she says in her sweet, shaky voice. Her big blue eyes blink up at me, and the girl who is normally a wild powerhouse of chaos looks so little, so vulnerable, lying there.

I squat beside her and push back her hair. "Don't you worry, babe. I'm just going to go wash your sheets and change my clothes, but I'll be right back out to have a cartoon marathon with you. Sound good?"

"Uh huh."

"Besides, Finley's here." I call him over from the overstuffed chair in the corner and he hops up onto the couch, lying down at Mila's feet.

She giggles at the sudden company. "Good boy, Fin-Fin."

After I strip her bed and toss the sheets and all the vomit-stained clothing into the wash, I sit down to give Ryan a call. I took care of Mom those few months of my senior year of high school before she died, but I've never tended a child who was sick.

He answers, his voice tired but sharp. "Hey, Kennedy? Everything okay?"

"Yes, but Mila's sick."

"Sick? Like, what are we talking?"

"I think she's got a fever, and she threw up a few times. I wouldn't have bothered you, but I wasn't sure what medicine, if any, to give her, or where your kids' thermometer is."

"Shoot, okay." In the background, I can hear a loud-speaker saying something about a Code Blue. "She can have ibuprofen or acetaminophen for the fever, but some kids can't tolerate even that when they're throwing up." Then he rattles off some other basic instructions for keeping her comfortable. "As for the thermometer, it's in the wall cabinet in my bathroom."

I mentally jot down everything he's said. "Okay. Got it."

"Are you sure? I can see about getting off early."

"Don't be silly. I've got this. If things get worse, I'll keep you posted."

Another code is called over the loudspeaker. "I'm so sorry, I have to go."

"Go save some lives, Dr. Ryan."

He chuckles. "But seriously, thank you, Ken."

"Any time."

"Okay." He pauses, like there's more he wants to say. "Bye."

It's deliciously awkward and I clutch the phone to my chest, sighing. How can just hearing his voice and talking about vomit make my pulse race?

I need to see that man again, STAT. But for now, I'll settle for getting a peek into his bedroom and bathroom, which I have never actually ventured inside despite having lived here for three weeks. (I know, it feels like a lot longer than that to me, too!)

I double-check on Mila again, but she's happily watching Daniel Tiger go on a family trip, so I move toward Ryan's room and push open the door. Even from the hallway, I can smell his handsome scent. (Can a scent be handsome? In this case, I vote YES.) His bedroom is about what I'd expect from him. Neat and tidy, with a king-sized bed to fit his tall frame, a large wood-stained headboard, and a gray and navy blue plaid comforter set. His furniture—which, aside from the bed, consists of a tall dresser and two side tables—is plain, sturdy, with no nonsense or frills. Then there's his bathroom—light and bright with marble countertops, but the cabinets are painted gray, which gives the whole bathroom a masculine vibe that's extremely attractive.

What's wrong with you, Kennedy? Being attracted to his bathroom. Get it together, woman.

But I don't care what my brain says. I'm gone over this guy, and I'm kind of tired of hiding it.

Mila calls for me from the other room, and I hurry to find the thermometer and the medicine Ryan mentioned in his cabinet. Then I hightail it back to the living room, to Mila, who is pale and crying again because she threw up in the bucket. I set the thermometer and meds on the table and deal with the mess.

All day long, this is how it goes, with occasional reprieves before more vomiting. When I check on Ava, she's having some gastro distress out the other end, but she doesn't want or need my help. Thankfully, Mila starts keeping down the meds and some water around seven at night, and Ava seems better then too. Hopefully this is just a twenty-four-hour thing, but just in case it isn't, I call Josh and let him know I can't work tomorrow. He says no problem and he hopes everyone feels better.

Now it's nine p.m. and I've finally made myself something to eat since the smell of anything when the girls were awake made Mila ill, and I honestly didn't have an appetite myself after cleaning up barf all day. But now that everyone is tucked away and Ryan has been updated with several texts that have gone unanswered, my stomach is severely protesting its emptiness.

Finley at my feet, I pop on some reality TV and am just lifting a bite of my sandwich to my mouth when the front door handle jiggles. I freeze but the dog jumps up, trotting to the archway that gives him a clear view of the front door. He must think it's Ryan, but Ryan isn't due home for ten or eleven more hours. So who is it? Should I call the police?

But then the door opens, and Finley's tail starts thumping the ground before he runs toward the intruder who must not be an intruder at all, given his reaction. I twist in my seat just as Ryan walks through the archway. "You didn't have to come home early. The girls are fine. I've got this handled. Did you not see my texts?"

"Watching *The Bachelor* without me again?" His voice is teasing, but there's something weak in his smile. And he didn't even address what I said, almost as if he didn't hear it.

It's then that I see the sheen of sweat on his face.

"Wait." I set down my dinner and hop up, rushing toward him. "Are you sick too?"

He hangs his messenger bag on a hook and leans heavily against the counter. "I think I might be."

And he definitely is. I press my hand against his forehead and he's hotter than Mila ever was. Grabbing the thermometer, I take his temperature and it registers a one-oh-two-point-seven. "How long have you felt like this?"

"I don't know. Most of the day. Since lunch for sure. But they … needed me." Then his eyes roll back in his head and I'm pretty sure this guy who weighs double what I do is about to faint.

"Ryan! Snap out of it."

His eyes flutter back open and he grins at me, a lazy out-of-it grin. "So … bossy."

I toss his arm around my shoulders. "Come on. Let's get you to bed." If he was any other guy, he might have cracked a joke at that one, but Ryan's mama raised him right. Either that, or he's just too far gone to register anything.

It takes a while, lots of heavy steps, and many uttered prayers, but we finally make it to his room, where he sits heavily on the edge of his bed and stares at the floor. Then before I can figure out a game plan here, he starts tugging off his shirt.

"Uh, what are you doing?"

His eyes narrow in concentration. How did this guy drive home without getting into an accident? Holy cow. "It's hot in here." And he whips off that shirt like it's nothing. I can't help but stare at the bulge of his biceps, the way his chest curves in all the right places, how his abs are distinct and countable. One, two, three …

Aaaaand I should probably stop ogling the half-naked sick man. "Do you need help?" At the way his head snaps back up to meet mine, my cheeks flood with heat. "I mean, with anything else? Can I get you anything?"

"No, I'm f—"

But he is not fine. Oh no. Not even a little. That poor man spends most of the night hugging the toilet, and I spend it by his side, patting his bare back, bringing him cool washcloths and water, which he says tastes good but then can't keep down. His fever eventually breaks around four a.m., and I get him back to bed after he takes a quick shower.

He falls right to sleep, and I start to leave. But what if he needs me again and is too weak to ask?

I shuffle down the hallway—So. Tired.—and check on Ava and Mila, who are still peacefully sleeping. Then I change into fresh yoga pants and a long-sleeved T and head back to Ryan's room, where I climb onto the opposite side of his bed. He's under the comforter so I stay on top of it. This should be all right. Totally appropriate, but efficient too.

Before I can think through the consequences of my actions, I shut my eyes and drift off dreaming of him.

fourteen

. . .

I MUST HAVE MADE a fatal error in the night—well, early morning. *Sometime* while I slept.

Because I am no longer on top of the comforter. Oh no. When my eyes open, I am underneath the sheets. And that wouldn't be so bad if my back wasn't pressed against Ryan's bare chest, his arm looped over my stomach, his steady breath warm on my neck, our feet tangled together at the bottom of the bed.

Oh my sheesh. This is … so toasty and snug. And comfortable. Do I really need to leave?

Yes. Because, thanks to Stomach Flu-Maggedon, Ryan and I haven't had a chance to talk about everything, and I don't want to get carried away with my feelings before that. Also because if Mila and Ava haven't already peeked in here and seen their nanny all curled up with their uncle, well, that's a scenario we should probably avoid.

Thanks to Ryan's blackout curtains (which I'm sure

come in handy when he's sleeping during the day and working overnights), I can't tell what time it is until I squint at the clock on the bedside table. Ten-eighteen. So we got about six hours of sleep. Not terrible considering the night we had. Ryan could definitely use even more to let his body recover.

I gently place my hand on his and—regrettably—lift it away from my waist, then scoot out from my spot and into a sitting position. I'm trying my best to be quiet, but just as I'm about to swing my legs toward my side of the bed, Ryan wakes and reaches for my arm. "Kennedy?"

"Hey," I whisper. "I'm just going to go check on the girls. You get some more sleep, okay? And let me know if you need anything else. I think the worst is over."

I'm not sure if what I'm saying is registering, because he's just blinking up at me, his eyes still soft with sleep. "You stayed."

So he noticed. "Um, yeah, I didn't mean to fall asleep in here, but I was worried you would need me and I wouldn't hear it from my room." I bite my lip. "Maybe I should have slept on the floor, but—"

"It's not that. I don't mind. It's just … I'm sorry you had to deal with that." He pushes up on one elbow. "And still you stayed."

"Of course I stayed. You were sick and needed me."

"A lot of women wouldn't have stayed."

Oh. Like Jillian. I tug on one of his curls and smile. "I'm not a lot of women."

"Don't I know it, darlin'."

Okay, what the what? I didn't think I could find Ryan's accent any more charming and then he goes and calls me *that*? Uh uh. It's an unfair advantage. Makes my inner vixen want to pounce and …

He needs to rest, Kennedy.

Ugh, fine. He does. I give him a pointed look and say, "Sleep," leaving the room with his chuckle in my ears. When I step out of the room and close the door, I lean back against it for support. Whew. The things that man does to my insides.

"What were you doing in Uncle Ryan's room?"

Ah! I jump at Ava's voice—and the teasing innuendo in it—and turn to find her sitting on the couch with Mila, each eating a bowl of cereal. Guess they're feeling better, thank goodness.

"He's sick too. I was checking on him."

Mila's totally engrossed in an episode of *Paw Patrol*, but Ava must hear the guilt in my voice. Because even though nothing happened, she doesn't know that, and I should have been more careful to set a good example for her—the kind I wish my mom had set for me.

Thankfully, she just tilts her head and taps her spoon against her ceramic bowl. "You took good care of all of us."

"It's my job, sweetie."

"It's more than that to you."

Oh my heart. I walk toward her and squeeze her shoulder. "You're right. I love you all very much."

"Even Uncle Ryan?" The tease is gone. It's a genuine question there.

I motion to the kitchen and she gets up to follow me, sliding onto a stool at the counter. After starting up the coffee machine, I make us both an Americano—apparently Ava likes them, and Ryan's said it's okay as an occasional treat. Then I pour some cereal for myself and sit beside Ava, who is hunched over her bowl. "What do you want to know?"

Her eyes widen. "You mean, you'll tell me? Even though I'm just a kid?"

"Ava, you're not just a kid. Sure, you're not an adult either, but if you don't learn to have honest conversations now, then your early adulthood will be a mess. Believe me." I take my mug in my hands and blow on the steam before taking a sip. Ah, the nectar of heaven, right here.

"Nobody's ever treated me like that. Except for Mom." Ava stirs the soggy Cheerios in her bowl. "Well, she doesn't really talk to me about stuff. More like treats me like an adult by leaving me to watch Mila all the time. When she goes out drinking."

Not the direction I thought this discussion was going to take, but I'll take any inroads I can get into Ava's mind and heart. "My mom didn't drink, but she started leaving me alone around age eight or nine to go out with different guys. Sometimes I'd be up until one in the morning waiting for her to come home, and eventually I would get so tired, I'd fall asleep." I haven't thought about that in a long time. The loneliness. The uncertainty. The fear that she'd gotten into an accident like the dad I barely remembered.

"That must have sucked."

"It did. It really did. And I'm sure it was terrible to be responsible for your sister when you were so young yourself." I breathe in the luscious scent of my brew—

rich and bold and beautiful. It brings strength to my mind and heart as I pray for the right words here. "I'm guessing you didn't tell anyone though, huh? Probably felt like it would be disloyal to your mom?"

"How did you know?"

"Because that's how I felt too. It was very lonely."

Her brow furrowed, Ava finally sips on her Americano, and her back straightens just a bit. "Uncle Ryan wants to help, but he's not very good about talking through things like this. And I don't want to hurt him, because my mom is his sister. He'd be super mad if he knew some of the things she'd done when she was wasted."

"You can always talk to me." How do I communicate the rest without making it sound like I'm on any side other than Ava's? I take a bite of cereal, crunch the round Os in my teeth, and wash it down with a swig of coffee. "But your uncle is trying because he loves you so much."

Ava's shoulders slump again and her chin trembles. "So if trying equals love, then why hasn't Mom tried? Really tried? To quit, I mean. Does that mean she doesn't ..."

"Oh, babe." I turn on my stool, and take Ava's hand in mine. "Look at me and listen up, okay? I don't know your mom, but I know this. There isn't a single person who really knows you who doesn't completely adore you."

She rolls her eyes, but I just squeeze her hand harder. She needs to believe this. "Ava Rosche, you are brave and fierce and funny and such a good big sister. Sometimes—a lot of times—we adults don't have it all together. Some things are bigger than us, and we need to get to a point where we are willing to ask for help. Your mom has a disease—"

"One she chose." She pulls back her hand and grabs up her spoon.

"I get how it seems like that. I do. Whatever made her start drinking, alcoholism is still a disease. A hard thing to conquer. But either way, no matter what happens with her, don't let your mother's choices change how you think about yourself."

The words I'm saying hit me full force. Oh wow. Okay. Um … hi. Biggest hypocrite in the world here. I blink back sudden tears. But I did promise honesty, didn't I? "That's something I'm still learning to apply in my own life. I just want to save you the time and energy."

She's quiet for a while, but I can tell she's thinking by the way her fingers squeeze and unsqueeze her spoon as she stares into her bowl. Then, "Thanks, Kennedy."

"Of course." My heart lifting at this unexpected opportunity to connect, I resume eating my cereal.

"So, when you and Uncle Ryan get married—"

I sputter out my bite, and turn a sharp eye on her.

She's grinning, and I can't help but laugh. "We aren't getting married." *Yet.*

Oh my. I really hope I didn't say that last part out loud.

But with the way Ava's eyebrows shoot sky-high, I'm guessing that maybe I did.

My mom used to read me that old poem about the walrus—the one who says it's time to talk of many things. Well, I don't need to talk about cabbages or kings, but if I don't say what I need to ASAP, I'm gonna burst.

I've been antsy for the last hour while putting Mila down to sleep for the night. She asked me to sing a trillion songs (fine, more like three) and read about a billion books (okay, five). Then she proceeded to ask a million questions (this might actually be accurate). But now, it's eight-thirty and the little angel (who spent much of today on the couch watching TV even though she felt better) is tucked in asleep and ready for a day of play tomorrow. Ava's in bed too, up reading the last time I checked.

I walk down the hall from Mila's room to the living room where I can hear the TV's muted tones. Ryan got out of bed around three and watched TV with the girls while I ran out to get some chicken soup for dinner. When I got back, we all ate together on TV trays and then I popped over to see Alexis since it's the end of her weekend. Thankfully, so far, the stomach bug has decided I'm not a good host, and you don't hear me complaining.

When I round the corner to the living room, I halt at the sight before me. Ryan and Finley are curled up on the couch together. Ryan is alert and his cheeks are no longer flaming and feverish like last night, but have a normal amount of color. He must have showered, because his hair is still damp and his clothes are different than earlier tonight—flannel pants and another hoodie that I hope to someday steal. There are two glasses of wine on the coffee table. All of this is quite normal.

What's not is his choice of entertainment.

"Watching *The Bachelor* without me?" I throw a hand on my hip with what I hope is an indignant look on my face.

He grabs the remote and pauses it, smiling. "I was just catching up on episodes you already watched." Then Ryan shifts, rubs the back of his neck. "You want to join me? We've got a finale to watch, don't we? Gotta find out how this thing ends."

Laughing, I plop onto the other side of Finley, who decides that three's a crowd and jumps down. Now there's just a cushion's worth of space between Ryan and me. I grab a blanket and toss it over my legs, which I curl up underneath me. "I have a confession to make."

"Oh yeah?"

I nod. "I actually know who won."

"I thought you hadn't watched it yet."

"Well, no, but these episodes are like ten years old. I follow the guy and his wife on social media. They've got the most adorable kids."

He shakes his head, chuckling. "What am I gonna do with you?"

That's the question, isn't it? My mind not at all on

reality TV, I blow out a breath. He seems to understand my change of thought, because he sets down the remote and turns to face me on the couch.

I turn toward him too, lay my head against the back couch cushion. And just like that, our knees are touching.

"Cold?" I ask him, holding up a corner of the blanket.

"Thanks." He takes it, and now we are sharing our warmth. Ryan drapes his arm across the back of the couch and his fingers fall just short of my face. "What's going on, Young'un?"

That makes me laugh just a little, enough to break the tension. "Are you up for talking? Or do you want to wait until you feel better?"

"I'm up for it if you are."

My fingers run along the woven threads of the red and black blanket. "I'm not really sure where to start."

"Why not start with what you want?"

Can I do that? *Be brave, Kennedy.* I peek up at him. "You," I whisper. "Us. This. But ..."

"But what, darlin'?"

If he was any other guy, he might take this opportunity to touch me, to sway my opinion. But he's just sitting there, giving me his full attention, but not pressuring.

And I kind of love him for it.

The thought threatens to make my insides explode. "I'm afraid."

He waits a few long moments before gently prompting me. "Of what?" It's crazy, how I can feel like his very voice is cradling me, holding me safely. Giving me room to speak my fears, but also reminding me that he's there.

"I'm afraid that I'll fall in love with you and you'll realize that I'm not what you want. My last boyfriend dumped me because I didn't want to go out every single night and I said *no* one too many times to what *he* wanted to do, and my mom got dumped once because she'd gained five pounds, and I've just never seen a healthy relationship play out from start to finish. I mean, my own father had another whole family when he met and got engaged to my mom. They never actually got married, because he was already married. Who *does* that?"

Ryan scoots forward at this declaration, his fingers brushing away the tears that are apparently falling down my cheeks. "I'm so sorry you went through all of that, Kennedy. You've been dealt some hard blows." He pauses. "Is Alexis—"

"The other daughter. Yeah. My half-sister." I choke out a bitter laugh. "We're like a regular soap opera. You really should run away now."

"In case you haven't noticed, I'm still sitting right here."

"For now. But what if this is just amazing in the moment, but goes downhill from here?" I know I shouldn't, but I lean into the warmth of his hand against my face. He stills my trembling chin with his thumb. "What if I disappoint you?" And now that the fears are bubbling out, I can't stopper them. They keep multiplying and coming, coming, coming. "If things don't work out between us, I'll lose both you *and* the girls."

Sometime during my rant, my fingers have fisted the blanket. I release it, smooth my palm down its rough surface. "I'm sorry. That was a lot." Too much, probably. Too much mess.

"Thank you for trusting me with all of that."

He's *thanking* me? That is the absolute last thing I expected. "I hope it doesn't sound like I think you're anything like Brooks. I know you're not. But I also wouldn't want to make you miserable."

"Kennedy, the last thing you'd make me is *that*. Don't you know how much joy you've brought back to this house? Laughter? And honesty. I'm not sure I've ever had such a frank conversation in all my life that doesn't revolve around medicine." Ryan tilts his head. "I told you. We need you. The girls *and* me."

My heart lifts at that heartfelt confession. "I need you too. Which is why I don't want to mess this up. If we think that this doesn't have the potential to go the distance, we should just stay friends, right? Because I can't afford to lose this job." Oh, that sounded bad. "And I'm not talking about finances. I'm talking about here." I press a hand against my chest.

"First of all, if you haven't gathered this yet, as far as I'm concerned, I want you to stay past the probation period. For the whole six months, if you're up for it."

That means more than words can say. But … "I'm still not completely decided." So much will depend on how this conversation goes.

"That's totally fine. You still have a week, and if you need more time, then take it."

Gran won't wait on her offer, so I can't really take more time anyway. But that's neither here nor there.

He continues. "Second, I hope you know that I would never fire you if we dated and broke up. Our status as a couple or not a couple in no way affects your job. Right now, I'm not your boss. In fact, I don't even really think of myself that way, ever. I think of you as my partner." Ryan's fingers move up my jawline to my ear, which he strokes from top to bottom as if it's the most fascinating part of my body. His eyes and his voice are filled with something like awe. "And third, I like you and want to be with you too. All of that stuff … it doesn't matter to me. It's made you the amazing woman you are. And do you know who that is, Kennedy?"

"Who?" My voice is hoarse, thick with emotion.

"You are so much more than the nanny. You are the woman who has captured my mind and heart from our very first meeting when you let my dog eat your pie."

I snort at the memory.

"But more than anything else, you are loyal. You"—he swallows hard, and I can see that this means more to him than all of the other stuff combined—"are someone who stays when she could have left. Just look at what you did for us this weekend."

"I would never have left you."

And I mean it. Not just because that would have been a rotten thing to do, but because even when he's throwing up and feverish, Ryan Rosche is still the sexiest and kindest man I've ever known. And I have a chance to make him mine … if I can brave my fears.

I tap his knee and he moves it down, shifting to face the TV so I can crawl up against him and snuggle under his arm, my feet pulled up and to the side. He adjusts the blanket so we are both covered and comfy.

Then Ryan grabs the remote and holds it. But before resuming the episode, he says, "Later this week, would you … can I take you out on a proper date?"

"You mean watching reality TV and drinking wine isn't proper?" I tease.

"It has its merits, and I foresee many, many nights like this in our future."

A thrill shoots up my spine at the confidence in his tone.

"But I've got something else in mind. Maybe Friday while the girls are at school?"

And I say the words I've been dying to say for weeks. "It's a date." Then I place my arm around his taut stomach and turn my attention back to the TV. I watch a man and a woman I've never met before get engaged. They're excited for what's to come, at the prospect of just doing life together.

Forever.

And for the first time, excitement beats out the fear when I think, *Someday, that could be me.*

fifteen

· · ·

IT'S BEEN the longest week of my life.

Five days might not seem like a lot, especially when they're filled with barista-ing and nanny-ing overnight and shuttling girls to their social worker appointments. But when you're waiting for Dr. Ryan Rosche to take you on what could be your last first date?

Yeah. They are as long as a flash sale is short.

But now, the morning has finally arrived. The girls are off to school, Chloe is all prepped to pick Mila up for me at two, and Ryan's been secretively ducking in and out of the house since I handed him his morning coffee with a hug and a smile.

All he told me is to wear "non-fancy jeans" (he's such a guy because what does that even mean?), a long-sleeved workout shirt, and closed-toe shoes that I "wouldn't mind getting dirty." I have no idea what he's got up his sleeves until I step outside at the appointed time.

When I see the two-seater ATV on the trailer that's hitched to the back of Ryan's truck, I cross my arms over my chest. "First you make me run. Please tell me you aren't also expecting me to get on that thing?" Of course, I'm teasing. In a recent *Bachelor* episode that we watched together after finishing the finale, one couple went four-wheeling and I exclaimed that I'd never done that but it looked fun.

Ryan was surprised, but looked secretly delighted despite his casual, *"Oh yeah?"*

Now, he's looking devilishly handsome and casual in his blue racing pants with a black, sweat-wicking, long-sleeved shirt. He tightens a strap over the ATV, securing it to the trailer, and man does his confidence and handiwork (and yes, MUSCLES) make my stomach flip. "Do you trust me?"

I laugh. "Okay, Aladdin." The sun is warm on my face and there isn't a single cloud dotting the horizon. It's going to be a beautiful day, and I can't wait to spend it with him.

"Ooo, nice," he says, moving toward me. "I figured that movie was too old for someone like you."

"It's a classic, I admit." I poke his ribs once he's in front of me.

Ryan grabs my hand and presses my palm flat against his chest. "You're killing me, Young'un."

Ooo, boy. How much I want to run my hand up the length of him, to tug him down to kiss me again. My lips have been aching to meet his all week long, to taste his again like they did ten days ago. But I've waited for a few reasons. One, because I've barely seen the man thanks to our work schedules. And two, because I wanted to separate Ryan the roommate-slash-boss from Ryan my date. The latter is the guy I want to kiss.

Maybe that sounds dumb. Obviously, they are all the same person. But I wanted to wait until we were away from the norm, away from our comfort zone, to make sure I felt the same magic with him that I do curled up on the couch or eating dinner together or helping with the girls.

So instead of taking his mouth captive in this moment, I just drop my hand and smile up at him. "But to answer your question, yes, I do trust you."

"Good. Then let's go."

We hop in the truck and I peek in the back seat, where there are several towels and blankets and a medium-sized cooler. What does this man have cooking? "I didn't even know you could four-wheel in San Diego."

"Yeah, there are several trails just outside the city. I used to go a lot on my days off." His hand is casually perched on the steering wheel as he pulls into traffic. "Reminds me of Oklahoma."

"Did you go a lot as a kid?"

He nods. "Our house was on some acreage in the country and my dad was big into it. And you know what they say—you can take the boy out of the country …"

And I have no desire to take the country out of the boy. Ahem. "It must be nice to have such wonderful memories of home. To have even *had* a real home growing up."

"You don't feel like you did?"

"We moved a lot. Lived with various boyfriends of my mom's. Lived with Gran for a time. But …"

"But?"

That night before we left—when I was hiding on the stairs and overheard the last time Mom and Gran ever spoke—will never leave my memory. "Let's just say that didn't work out."

Ryan must be able to sense that I don't want to ruin today with talk of Gran, so he moves the conversation to my job at Java Awakening. We chat about various things while Lady A plays on the radio as we leave the city and drive toward the mountains just east of San Diego. After about an hour, we head into the national forest and eventually pull up to a trailhead. There are a few other vehicles there, but mostly, the place is deserted. It's quiet and peaceful, the air punctuated by the call of a hawk, the scurry of a lizard across the dirt path that winds up from the trailhead.

This isn't like any national forest I've been in before. No towering trees—more like a desert with greasewood shrubs taller than I am, but also some unusual and really cool rock formations in the distance.

We get out of the truck and Ryan snatches a few things from the back seat of the cab. He meets me near the ATV and hands me a hot pink racing jacket. "I know how much you like wearing my clothes, but I thought it might be dangerous if you wore something so big."

He helps me put the jacket on—because he's the perfect gentleman—and it's an exact fit. "Who'd you borrow this from?"

"It's yours to keep." And he doesn't have to say it for me to think it … that maybe this won't be the last time we do this together.

"Well, thank you. You're really nailing this date thing."

Winking at me, he slips on his own jacket. "I plan to make this a day you'll never forget, Young'un."

Oh, I sure hope so. "Bring it on, Old Man. Though now that I think of it, are you sure this is safe for someone your age? I hear when you reach thirty, your body starts to fall apart." I blink innocently at him.

His eyes laughing, he leans in close. "My body works *just* fine. You'll see."

Shivers dance up my arms, and I know it's not the crisp breeze kicking up and blowing circles in the brush.

While Ryan gets the ATV unloaded and all ready to go, setting the cooler on the back rack behind the passenger seat, I take photos of the surrounding area. The ground still has some muddy spots from the rain we had earlier this week. Maybe that's what the towels in the truck are for—when we inevitably get splattered with mud.

And why do I suddenly understand the appeal of Brad Paisley's song *Mud on the Tires* with new eyes?

Whew. Sticking my phone into a zippered pouch in my jacket, I start to fan myself. Maybe I should peel this jacket off. It's getting hot out here.

"You ready?" Ryan approaches with eye goggles and a helmet that he hands to me.

"I think so. What do I need to know?"

After he explains the safety basics of riding on the ATV, I put on my eyewear and helmet. Then he gives me a hand up onto the contraption and climbs on in front of me. The back seat sits slightly above his so I can see around him even though he's so tall. I've got hand grips on either side of my hips, and though I'm kind of bummed I don't get to live out the fantasy of holding him around the waist while we ride, the logical part of me can see how this is much more secure. Also, my head won't bang into his back whenever we go over bumps.

And bumps, we definitely go over.

Once he makes sure I'm good, he revs the engine and takes off down the trail, slowly at first and then picking up speed. The trail curves this way and that. It's fairly flat terrain, but the brush rises on either side of us, making me feel both small and important—after all, it's like the land is rolling out the red carpet, allowing us to cut straight through its heart, to experience all the freedom life has to offer.

We bounce and jostle, but the ATV can handle it—and boy, can Ryan handle the ATV. He's an expert at the twists and turns, and it only makes him sexier, especially when he whoops and hollers as we bounce through mud puddles and ground that's eroded away, making it rough and uneven. I giggle and shout along with him, because this is just plain fun.

No expectations of me. I'm not performing or being judged on my performance. We are just two people, letting loose, all of our responsibilities checked at the trailhead.

We've been riding for quite some time when we round a bend and I gasp at the scenery—a green and white and blue sort of wilderness stretching out beyond the place where we sit at a higher elevation than I realized. It strikes me as mostly untouched by humanity. There's something pure and strong about it, maybe. Something that calls to me.

The wind whistles freedom through its crags and trees.

Ryan pulls up to an outcropping and turns off the engine. Then he swings his leg over and helps me down from my seat too. My feet are unsteady for a few moments, and he grabs my waist. "It'll take just a second to adjust to being on solid ground again."

I take off my helmet and goggles, set them down. "Got it." Our clothes are splattered with mud—not coated, but just enough that someone looking on would know we'd just had an adventure.

"So what'd you think?" Pulling off his goggles and helmet, Ryan runs a hand through his curls. His cheeks are flushed. Alive.

"I think that was even more fun than *The Bachelor* made it look." I smile. "Honestly, the best part was seeing you let loose. You're always so serious. It was nice to see you relax and have fun."

"Four wheelin' has a way of doing that." He unstraps the cooler from the back rack of the ATV, and peeks up at me. "So does being with you, darlin'."

Before I can respond, he moves the cooler—and a plastic-wrapped blanket that's underneath it—to a dry spot on the ground that's got an amazing view. Though, honestly, everywhere up here seems to.

I unzip my jacket and pull out my phone, snapping some shots. "Come here."

Eyebrow raised, he obeys, and when I lift the phone for a selfie, he moves in close, pressing our cheeks together. I take some pictures of us with the amazing background. "Okay, now would you mind taking a few pics of me on the ATV? Alexis will never believe the city girl did something like this without proof."

Laughing, he takes the phone and backs up while I climb onto the rack where the cooler was just sitting. I pose, my arms lifted like I'm a muddy Vanna White. Once he's taken a few pictures, he brings my phone back to me. "Did I do okay? I'm not much good at taking photos."

I look at the first shot and can't keep the grin off my face. I'm surrounded by nature, looking like a proper country girl with a bit of city pizzazz in my demeanor. And there is Ryan's finger making a smudge in the upper right corner. "It's perfect." I stuff the phone back into my inner jacket pocket.

I'm about to ask what he packed for lunch, but then I look up to find Ryan still standing there, just watching me. "What?"

"*You're* perfect." He moves closer, and reaches up to rub something off the side of my jaw. "Even with mud on your face."

I've stopped breathing. What is air? What is oxygen? Do I really need those? My lungs don't think so. And words. Those are failing me too.

Especially when Ryan places his hands on my thighs —steadying me as I balance on the edge of the seat, but also giving my whole body wings to fly away. His thumbs brush from side to side. Such tiny movements shouldn't have the power to set my entire body aflame. I mean, he's not even touching my skin.

And yet.

"I'm not perfect," I finally manage. "Far from it."

"You're perfect for *me*. Maybe not on paper, necessarily. You're so sophisticated, with your fancy coffees and clothes that look like they belong on a runway."

I want to roll my eyes, tell him I'm just a normal girl. But I'm frozen. Utterly and completely. He's Jack Frost and I'm his oh-so-willing victim.

"I didn't think you and I would have anything in common," he continues. "I mean, what would you want with a country boy? But here you are, muddy on the back of an ATV. I think there's a little bit of country in you after all, Kennedy Matkin." He shifts, so his lips are hovering over my ear. "And can I just tell you something?"

I shiver and slink my hands around his neck and up into his curls—just as thick and luxurious as I imagined them to be. "What's that?" I whisper.

His lips graze my earlobe. "I've never been more attracted to you than I am right now."

Oh. My. Gaaaaaaaaaaah.

"I'm more attracted to *you* than I've ever been to anyone." I swallow, my throat as dry as the wind chapping my cheeks. "But … I'm still scared." Of losing him. Of losing the girls. Of losing the first sense of self, of home, that I've truly had in … well, maybe ever.

Ryan pulls back, looks me dead in the eyes. His eyebrows furrow. "I'm scared too. Scared to fail you. Scared that giving into this want—this craving I have for you—will somehow chase you away, which will mean failing the girls. But I keep coming back to this idea that maybe we are stronger together than we are apart."

Oh, please, let him be right.

Before I can respond, he continues. "But if you ever decide that you don't want this, I respect that."

I cock my head, bite my bottom lip—an action his eyes seem to zero in on. "I want this more than I've ever wanted anything." A tear escapes my eye and I look away, briefly. Bring my gaze back to his. "You surprise me at every turn, Dr. Ryan."

"I hope that's a good thing, darlin'."

"It's the best thing." I tilt my chin up. "And I hope the surprises just keep coming."

That's all the invitation he needs. Before I can think or breathe or feel anything else, he's kissing me. And oh, it is glorious. His lips are the home I've been missing, that I've been searching for all these years. But this is not a cuddle-up-on-the-couch-and-watch-TV kind of kiss. It's not a gentle press of the lips, a greeting, a casual hello or goodbye.

It's a hold-on-for-all-you're-worth explosion, a volcano that decimates a landscape so there can be new growth. It's paving the way for all the kisses that have yet to be. I've never experienced anything like it, and yet, now that it's here, now that it's mine, I know it well.

I know him well—I know *us*.

I know Ryan's hand, wrapped tight around my waist, skimming the skin just under my shirt, gliding across my lower back. And I know his other hand plunging into my hair, massaging my head with his strong fingers.

I know his mouth on mine, the taste of his mint toothpaste on my tongue, his warm breath skating across my jaw. I know my gasp when his lips hit the hollow beneath my ear.

I know his tongue, flitting across my feverish skin, and my hands tugging him closer, my chin lifting to give him better access. My legs, looped around his waist, so if he wanted to hold me fully, all he'd need is to place his hands under me and lift me off of this ATV.

I know the burn of his five o'clock shadow on my jaw, my neck, as he explores every exposed inch of my skin with his lips. I know his frustrated growl when he reaches my clavicle, which disappears beneath my shirt, stopping him from continuing his trek downward.

I know his groan when I angle my head upward and kiss a ring around the shell of his ear. When I nibble his earlobe. When I bring our lips together again in a burst of playful teasing, flitting away as he chases me, then giving in to his mouth's every demand.

I know my hands lowering to his broad chest. His heart beating unevenly beneath my fingertips. I know our breaths, converging, wild and erratic in their singularity.

I know our want, our desires pulsing and prodding, seeing how far they can push us without breaking us in the process.

And I know, as Ryan Rosche kisses me, pulling me apart and putting me back together over and over, that I will never be the same again.

sixteen

. . .

THE DEADLINE TO tell Gran whether I want the marketing job is still two days away.

But I don't need to wait—I know what I want. My certainty is solidified during the rest of our date, during the drive home, during the kiss Ryan gives me on the darkened front stoop before we step inside to find a very smug-faced Chloe waiting for us, the girls already in bed.

During the entire next day, which we spend shopping at Liberty Station and doing workshops with the girls—me and Mila at a ceramics class and Ryan and Ava at a woodworking class.

And now tonight, when Ryan sneaks a kiss in the hallway before slipping into Mila's room to put her to bed.

It's time to face Gran—to put all the *what-if*s behind me for good. Phone in hand, I turn and nearly scream when I see Ava there, arms folded over her chest and an "I told you so" look on her face.

She must have seen Ryan and me kissing.

Oops.

"Uh, hi."

"Hi, yourself," she says. "Looks like *yet* is getting closer, huh?"

"I don't know what you're talking about." As I move past Ava, I throw a hip bump her way.

"Sure you don't." She giggles. "When can I start calling you Aunt Kennedy?"

My bare feet trip over themselves and I grab the archway column to steady myself. How have I never thought about this—that if things work out between Ryan and me, these girls will become my family? Before she can run away, I turn and take this scrawny preteen into my arms.

She squeaks out a protest, but after a minute, relaxes into my hold—and wraps her arms around my waist.

We don't say anything more, but we don't have to. Somehow, this girl I've only known for a month has become a beautiful, wonderful part of my life.

And I might not have to lose her when this nanny gig is up after all.

I kiss the top of her hair and she pulls her head away, but the look in her eyes tells me it's just for show. If she gave into what she really wanted, she'd keep letting me hold her. This poor girl has been missing a mother's touch for a long time. And I'm no mother, but my heart wants to protect her. Her and Mila.

And I don't think there's anything more maternal than that.

"All right," I finally say, dropping my hold and giving her space. "Off to bed with you."

"I just want to say I think it's really lame I have a bedtime on a Saturday. It's only nine."

I tap my chin. "You're right. Why don't you queue up a movie out here, then? I need to make a quick call, but we can have a girls' night if you'd like. Find a good chick flick."

"Really?" Ava tugs at her hair. "What about Uncle Ryan?"

"He'll survive."

"Maybe he would want to join us?"

I don't want her thinking that my affection for her is only based in what I feel for her uncle. "It's up to you."

"Okay." And then she does it—full-on smiles. It's blinding and brilliant and the most welcome sight in the world. "I'll pop some popcorn."

"Great." I lean in and whisper. "I hid some M&Ms on the top shelf of the pantry. Why don't you grab those too?"

"Will do." Then she walks toward the kitchen, while I steel myself for what's to come.

The temperature dropped today thanks to a brief storm this morning, so before heading for the backdoor, I reroute to my room and grab Ryan's hoodie out of the closet. When I tug it on, I pull the front lip over my nose and give a good sniff. Ah. That's the best smell in the world. It'll be like he's standing right beside me as I talk to Gran—as I face my doom.

Most people probably wouldn't call their grandmothers at nine o'clock, but this is Martha Montgomery we're talking about. The woman is a machine, and she never goes to sleep until midnight.

And I don't want to wait another day to tell her my decision. Not because I'm afraid I'll change my mind, but because I need this to be behind me. I want nothing more than to look into my future and see only good things—not the dread, the ball in the pit of my stomach, that I do right now.

I slide open the door and step out into the crisp air. Finley follows me and immediately races off to a corner of the yard, barking at some unseen animal. Next door, Alexis's house is party central, with music going and figures standing at the kitchen windows. She and Dax invited me over via text, but I said I had plans tonight. Somehow, she saw through my flimsy excuse and asked me when I was going to properly introduce Ryan to her —as if she knew that things had changed between us. Maybe Chloe blabbed about our date, or maybe the fact that she (and Tia … sort of) babysat the girls all afternoon gave it away.

Whatever she knows or doesn't know, I'm not really afraid to tell her about Ryan and me. Not after the conversation we had at the karaoke bar. Since then, she's been softer, more supportive, less likely to blurt out her judgments. (I mean, I've only really seen her once or twice in passing, but STILL. She's trying.)

That is not likely to be my experience with Gran, though.

Ugh. I just need to get this over with. *No more stalling, Kennedy.*

With trembling fingers, I dial and Gran's terse "Hello" comes within mere seconds. "Hey, Gran." I force a chipperness I do not feel into my voice. "How are you doing?"

"Kennedy Montgomery Matkin, I'm working, and you know how much I despise chitchat." I can picture her rubbing her wrinkle-free temple like she always does when she's frustrated. "Get on with the reason you called."

"Okay." Some kind of bugs click in the yard beyond the concrete slab where I'm standing. I stamp my feet to warm them up. "While I'm very grateful for the job offer you've extended to me, I've decided that I'm not going to take you up on it."

"I see."

For some, silence is uncomfortable. But for Gran, it's a weapon. And she's got a black belt in using it.

Just hang up. "All right, well, that's all I had to—"

"It's because of that boy, isn't it?" Her tone drips with derision.

I'm not going to dignify that with a response. Because it's about so much more than just Ryan, but how can she possibly understand? She only ever saw my mom in black and white too—in the things she liked and didn't like.

One far outweighed the other.

My insides ache, but the light from the house streams out through the windows and door, cloaking me with strength. There are people in there who love and accept me for who I am. I do not have to dwell in the darkness of the ones who don't. "That's my decision, Gran. I'm not going to change it. Goodn—"

"Wait." She clucks her tongue. "I have another offer for you."

There's something almost desperate in the way she says it. Or maybe I'm just reading into things. Still, it doesn't hurt to hear her out. "What offer?"

"I'll wait one more month. Then I'm posting the job."

"Gran, my current job commitment goes through July."

"What if I sweeten the pot?"

She's already planning to pay me enough for an entire year of school within the first three months. What else could possibly make this a better gig?

"Come to work for me starting April first. Once you've been here for three months, I will hand over your trust fund in its entirety."

My heart drops to my frozen toes. Finley's barking is a distant rattling in my ears. My entire trust fund? That's over a million dollars. The things I could do with that money … I'd have time to figure out what I wanted to do, to pay for college, to invest in a solid future.

But … no. I can't leave Ryan and the girls. Not now. They need me. And I need them more than I need a million dollars.

"Gran, I—"

"I've got to go. Think about what you want to do and let me know by March 15." Then the line goes dead and my phone screen goes black.

Holy sheesh.

Before I have a moment to gather my thoughts, the backdoor slides open and Ryan steps out. "Hey, darlin'. What are you doing out here?"

"Just making a call."

Finley runs up to greet Ryan and he gives him a vigorous pat before walking up to me and wrapping me in a bear hug from behind. "Everything okay?"

I place my hands on his forearms and snuggle back against his solid chest. "Just spoke to Gran." I've told him a little bit about her and the dynamic we had growing up. "I turned down a job opportunity she's been trying to get me to take."

"What job?"

"One that would require me to move to San Francisco, work with my ex-boyfriend, and be under her thumb for the rest of my life."

"Sounds thrilling."

"Doesn't it, though?" I chuckle, but the sound is hollow in my throat. Tonight the clouds obscure the moon, and the scraggly trees in Ryan's yard cast shadows across the grass. "I could tell she wasn't happy when I turned her down. She even tried to bribe me with my trust fund."

"Trust fund?"

"Yeah. She set it up for me when I was little. But it's not a normal trust fund, where I get it when I turn a certain age. No, it's attached to me satisfying her requirements."

"Such as?"

"Just generally doing whatever she wants me to do. But I've been a grave disappointment so far. Frankly,

I've been a disappointment since the moment I was born out of wedlock to a mother she already didn't approve of."

"Surely she can't fault *you* for that."

I shrug. "She sure holds it against me, though. She thinks the only way to redeem the way I came into the world is by becoming 'more Montgomery' and 'less Matkin.'" The words turn acrid on my tongue. "Can you believe that when I was around Ava's age, I heard her tell my mom that she was doing a terrible job with me? That I was turning out just like her. That just like her, I was going to end up a slu—" My lips seal shut. "I can't even say the word."

"You don't have to, darlin'. Because none of that's true—especially the part about being a disappointment." Ryan kisses my cheek, so soft and sweet that I want to cry. "She's blind if that's what she sees when she looks at you."

I squeeze his arms. "I think you might be a little blind yourself."

"Nah, I see well for the first time in a long time." He clears his throat. "So … have you considered her new offer?"

What? I rear back and twist so I can look at him. "Why would I do that? Didn't you hear how terrible she's been to me?"

His hands fall to my waist. "I know." Ryan grimaces. Blinks. There's something there, behind his eyes, but he's hiding it from me. Trying, at least. What is he thinking? "But your trust fund isn't something you should give up lightly."

Oh, Ryan. "I don't see it as giving something up. I see it as choosing something different." Even without the moonlight, I can see his jaw tick. I reach up my hand and rub the spot. "I made a commitment to see this through with the girls."

"Ken, I don't …" He swallows hard, looks away. "I don't want to hold you back. You could do a lot with that money."

"I know. But I don't need it."

He huffs out a breath. "You're not thinking clearly about this." Is he exasperated at me, or the situation? "Give it a little time before you decide."

Why is he saying this? "I don't need time. For the first time, I know what I want." I go up on my tiptoes and kiss him soft on the mouth, then pull back. "You."

"Don't give this up for *me*. I'm not worth all that."

"First of all, you totally are." I smooth my fingers across his jaw, his neck. He swallows hard against my touch. "And second of all, I'm not giving it up for you. I'm giving it up for me."

And there's a peace I've never known that comes with it.

A surety that I am exactly where I'm supposed to be.

seventeen

. . .

THERE'S a certain magic in the air when winter turns over into spring. Maybe it's just the blossoming of new life on the trees, the twittering of birds and animals waking up from a long slumber, the sun's rays staying a little longer each day.

But for me, this spring is the most magical of all, because in the two weeks since Ryan and I went on our date, *I've* felt new. I am no longer the woman afraid to give her heart.

And my sister has noticed.

"You seem different." Alexis and I stroll through the K-8 school parking lot, which is currently the site of a good old-fashioned spring carnival. It must have taken a ton of volunteers, time, and effort to plan this thing, with its rows and rows of games like the balloon pop, the bottle toss, and boat races, as well as booths for face painting and silly photos. Food truck vendors line the front of the school, and the smell of everything from hot dogs to fried Twinkies permeates the Saturday night air. In the far corner of the lot, a Ferris wheel gleams, reflecting the light from lamps that obscure the stars I know must be up in the clear velvet sky tonight.

"Do I?" I loop my arm through hers. Ryan is here somewhere with the girls, so I'm off nanny duty for the night. I'm planning to join them later, but Alexis requested a few minutes of solo sister time. (We did a double date last weekend, but haven't spent time just the two of us for a while.) We did dinner out and then came here together, since she and all her friends were already coming to the carnival tonight in a show of support for Shelby, who—poor thing—was appointed to be the teacher in charge of this event. I can't imagine planning this in addition to her wedding, which is supposed to take place in July. "Is that a bad thing?"

"No." Alexis tosses her brown braid over her shoulder. It's still strange seeing her without her bright hair, but now and then she switches back to her natural color. (I think Dax likes it. Calls it her "non-poopy" hair color. Not sure what that's about.) "You're—I don't know. More confident, maybe? I mean, you've always been confident in your style and appearance, that sort of thing. But now you seem more assured in who you are. In your decisions. Like how you decided to apply for school here in San Diego and pursue social work. I didn't see that coming, but it totally fits you."

"Thanks. That means a lot. To be honest, I didn't see it coming either." But when I last took the girls to an appointment with their social worker, I observed how gentle, how kind, their case worker was. And when I asked her if she'd mind me picking her brain about the profession, and she agreed to go to coffee with me, and then answered all of my questions, I got this feeling in my gut. Something definitive. Something almost divine.

When I ran the idea past Ryan—still unsure that the girl who had messed up so badly in the past could do any real good in the world—his face lit up. He told me that I'd be an amazing asset to all the hurting kids out there.

His belief in me gave me the courage to move forward and submit an application to San Diego State. I'm still waiting to hear whether I got in, but the counselor I met with didn't seem to think it would be a problem, especially with the note of explanation I gave as to my last foray into—and exit from—college.

"Ryan seems to be good for you."

My stomach growls as we pass a popcorn truck. "You think so?" I mean, I definitely do. We've both had to work a lot of days lately, but have spent our evenings wrapped up in each other, talking about everything under the sun, snuggling in between episodes of *The Bachelor*—and a few action movies like he prefers—and, of course, kissing.

So. Much. Kissing.

And I am here for it. Ryan's kisses have a way of making me forget where we are. Of course, with the girls being just down the hall, we haven't gotten too carried away. But there was that one time Mila sleep-walked into the living room while we were making out on the couch and nearly scared us to death.

Life with kids, am I right?

"Yeah, I do." She hugs my arm against her body and redirects me toward the picnic tables that are set up for people who are eating. "The thing is, love changes you. It makes you do crazy things. And that can be a good thing or a bad thing. With Stooks"—her lip curls—"your love for him made you only half of yourself. You hid away what you wanted. I think I did the same with Corbin." She rarely talks about her ex, but I squeeze her arm back in acknowledgment of the pain that guy caused her. "But true love with the right man—a man who is strong enough to handle a woman with her own opinions and desires—"

"Like Dax?" I hip bump her.

"We're talking about you right now." A smirk flits across her lips. "But yes. That man drives me absolutely insane, but I love him so much it scares me sometimes."

Ah, Sis. "I'm happy for you, A."

"And I'm happy for you. Because from what I've seen so far, being with Ryan has made you braver, able to speak your truth without fear that he's going to leave you. He seems like a really good man."

"He is." And suddenly, my heart aches to find him. I think he said he had been wrangled into volunteering for a booth—but which one? Was it the fishing game? The balloon pop? I'm not sure even he knew.

"Good. Because I told him when we hung out last week that if he hurts you, he's gonna have to answer to me. And I don't mess around when it comes to my little sister."

I laugh, then pull her to the left to sidestep a toddler running from his mother. There must be a thousand or more people moving among the booths. "So what you're saying is, you were wrong."

She flashes me a confused look. "About what?"

"About how moving in with Ryan and becoming the girls' nanny was the dumbest idea I ever had. Remember that?" I ask in a singsong voice.

Alexis rolls her eyes and grits her teeth. The woman hates admitting defeat. "Fine. I was wrong."

"Can I get that on video?" a teasing voice says in front of us.

Laughter explodes from several people.

I look up and find an entire picnic table filled with familiar faces—namely Dax, who is lounging backward and looking at Alexis with lifted eyebrows and a glint of humor in his eyes. Beside him sit Chloe and Tia, and Evie, Lauren, and Kayla are across the stretch of table. Josh and Connor stand next to each other, each with a baby strapped to their chests like some sort of Baby-wearing Bro Club. Shelby and Eric must be around here on duty somewhere. In fact, I saw him rush by earlier saying something into a walkie-talkie about an over-flowing porta-potty.

"You wish." Alexis moves forward quickly to greet Dax, who stands and gives her a kiss that lasts a bit longer than comfortable.

"Get a room!" Connor shouts. Evie spears him with a look that indicates she disapproves … but also finds him amusing.

Clearly unphased, Dax breaks the kiss and then turns to face the group again, draping his arm over Alexis's shoulders. "So, we eating soon or what?"

Alexis pats his stomach. "Always hungry."

He whispers something into her ear and she smacks him. Don't wanna know what that was about.

"Kennedy." Chloe lifts her hand. "You're finally showing your face. I thought perhaps Ryan was keeping you captive in that house."

"Ryan was doing *something* with her in that house," Kayla jokes.

And now it's Josh's turn to shake his head at his significant other. "What are we gonna do with you, Leia?"

Grinning, she blows him a kiss. "Don't worry, Han. She knows I'm kidding."

In the wake of my friends' teasing laughter, I turn back to Chloe. "Ha ha. I do live there, you know. It's perfectly reasonable for me to be there a lot."

"Just be sure to come up for air every once in a while or we'll have to send the bobbies in for a welfare check." She winks at me. "Now come and join us." The princess pats the seat beside her that Dax just vacated.

Groaning, I fold my hands together in apology. "I can't. I told Ryan I'd come and find him."

After more teasing, I finally make my way to the preschool section of the carnival, with tamer games aimed at younger kids. A brief glance at my phone doesn't show a text from him, so I'm not sure exactly where he is.

Until I spot a gaggle of women with their littles.

They're crowded around a booth that doesn't look all that interesting—a lollipop tree. Given the fact that most of the other booths have only a few kids waiting in line, you'd think this was the big showstopper booth. But come on. The lollipop tree? From what I understand, some lollipops have black dots on the bottom of them. If a child chooses that one, they get an extra lollipop as a prize. Nothing high stakes or showstopping about it.

Then I see who is working the lollipop tree. And it all makes sense what—or rather, who—is stopping the show.

My man is squatting beside an adorable little boy in suspenders and a bow tie whose face is screwed up as he considers allllll the options. Ryan's attention is fully on the child.

And all of the moms' attention is fully on him.

Oh brother. Some of them look older than him, but most are probably his age. I've seen several of them at pickup. There are a few without wedding rings on (some even with!), and all of their hair and makeup are flawlessly done. And they are hankering for something other than lollipops at the moment.

Too bad for them, because as soon as the boy chooses his lollipop, Ryan stands and catches sight of me. A huge grin greets me—and many frowns from disgruntled women who are upset that he's looking at someone other than them that way. But despite how beautiful each one of them is, he only has eyes for me.

And that's something I'll never get over.

"Hey." He hugs me and gives me a kiss on the cheek. "Thanks for coming."

"Of course." I glance around. "Where are the girls?"

"Marilyn stopped by and asked if she could take them around."

"Ah." So time alone? I love the girls, but I will always take that. "When are you off here?"

He checks his watch. "Maybe five minutes?"

"Great. I'll help."

We work the booth together, though upon my arrival—and our obvious togetherness—the crowd thins considerably. About ten minutes later, one of the preschool teachers approaches and says she's there to take over.

And then Ryan's got me by the hand and is pulling me across the lot like something's on fire.

"Ryan?" We're approaching the backside of the school building. "Everything okay?"

"It is now." He tugs me into an alcove—a dark alcove where there is no one else. "I missed you."

I can't help the giggle that escapes my throat. "I missed you too." My back presses against the building wall.

Ryan places a hand on either side of my head. I love how his frame towers over me. "Hi," he says.

"Hi." And with that, I grab a fistful of his T-shirt and tug him forward.

One of his hands falls to my hip and then he leans down and kisses me. It's not the frantic kiss like many we've shared as of late. This kiss is sensual, heated but slow and deep, like I'm a dessert that he's savoring one luscious bite at a time. He's still not near enough for my liking, so I manage to find the belt loops of his jeans and draw his body even closer. His strength could easily overpower me, but Ryan is the gentlest giant I've ever known. And I honestly can't get enough of him.

I sigh into his kiss, and this seems to ignite something in him. His hand flexes on my waist, and his mouth moves to his favorite spot—okay, mine too—on my neck. And he's downright worshipful in his attention.

But before he can showcase his full reverence, the ringtone on his phone pierces the night.

He groans and pulls back a tad. "Sorry. I flipped it on so Marilyn could get ahold of me."

"No problem." My heart is erratic in my chest, and I brush my hands through my hair while Ryan pulls his phone from his back pocket and checks the caller ID.

He frowns.

"What is it?"

"I think Sophie's calling me." He blinks. "She usually calls on Sundays. Something might be wrong."

"Answer it." I tilt my head. "Do you want me to stay?"

"You can if you want." Ryan runs a hand through his hair. "Or I can come find you when I'm done."

I can't read him, and I definitely don't want to intrude. "I'll just meet you over there, at the edge of the preschool area. There's a bench."

"Okay." He turns from me and holds the phone up to his ear. "Hello?"

Head down, I start walking but not before I hear him say, "Wait, what?"

Everything in me wants to know what's going on. What if something happened to Sophie? She could be sick—or worse. I clutch my stomach, praying for Ryan and the girls' sake that nothing is wrong. That Sophie just decided she needed to hear her brother's voice.

My gut tells me it's more. But my gut has been wrong before.

I find the bench and pull out my phone, aimlessly scrolling social media for half an hour. I cross and uncross my legs, my foot bouncing. The carnival swirls around me, happy noises, happy kids, but with every second that Ryan's gone, my stomach twists tighter. I glance back into the darkness, squint, but I can't even make out the shadow of him.

Should I seek him out?

But no. He's a grown man, and he said he'd come and find me. Ryan's a man of his word. So, I bury my nose in my phone and wait, trying to ward off the worry that's threatening to steal my joy.

And then, at last, he's there, sliding onto the bench beside me. "Hey."

"Hey." I twist my body toward Ryan's, so our knees touch.

He's got a blank look on his face, his jaw is clenched, and his shoulders are stooped. He props one elbow onto the back of the bench and leans his head into his palm.

"What's going on? Is Sophie okay?"

"She's … better than okay, actually. I guess rehab is going well, and she's looking into taking college classes when she gets out. Maybe becoming a nurse."

Oh. "Well, that's great." I place my hand on his knee. "Why don't you sound happy then? Are you just afraid she's going to relapse again?"

He lifts his head, sighs. "There's always that possibility. It's happened so many times before. Makes it hard to believe that she'll ever change, though I want that so badly for her. For the girls."

"Of course you do." I rub my thumb over Ryan's kneecap. "But remember. You aren't responsible for her recovery or her decisions."

He opens his mouth to reply, but a family of four walks by, one child thrashing in his dad's arms, screaming, "But I want cotton caaaaaandy!" at the top of his lungs. His baby sister is crying from her place in the stroller, which the mom is pushing at top speed toward one of the exits.

Once we're relatively alone again, he continues, a frown fixed on that handsome face. "I know it's not my responsibility, but if she relapses again, then what happens to the girls?"

"*If* that happens, then you'll be there to help again. And so will I."

His arm comes around my shoulders then and he pulls me close, kissing my temple. "That might be kind of hard given my sister's latest scheme."

"What scheme?"

"She wants to move them to Oklahoma. Can you believe it? Says she still has a few friends in the town we used to live in. You know, the town she hated and couldn't wait to get away from."

"Maybe she sees the merits of small-town living now. You said yourself it's a great place to raise kids."

"That's what she says, but I know her. She hates being bored. Most likely, she'll end up living in the city

—especially if she's serious about school, since my alma mater is right there in Norman."

"That wouldn't be so bad, would it? It might help give her some direction, a better way to support the girls."

"You're right. School would be good for her, but it's stressful. And stress is a trigger for someone with an addiction." His voice sounds more and more frantic.

"Hey." I snuggle against him, place my hand over his heart. "We'll figure this out."

"I already have."

There's something strangled in his tone. Sorrowful. Apologetic. I sit up and twist so I can see his face. "Oh?"

"Kennedy, if my sister moves … I have no choice but to move with her. To help her with the girls."

I blink. He's thinking about leaving? "Ryan, you have a choice. You always have a choice." My heart is unsure what to do right now—it alternately flutters and halts, like a manual car sputtering uphill in the wrong gear. Of course I want to encourage him to take care of his family, but what about us?

No, this isn't even about us. It's about him and his incessant savior complex. He's a good man, but he's just a man. Doesn't he see that?

I fold my lips inward, over my teeth. Then, "Ryan, this is a non-issue. There are still three months until she gets out of jail. She'll probably change her mind by then."

"I don't know. I think she's pretty serious. And when she gets an idea in her head … watch out."

"But she didn't *ask* you to go with her, did she?"

"Not in so many words. But how can I not? She's gonna need help."

"Then she shouldn't move away from the only support system she and the girls have. It's selfish, is what it is." There. I said it.

He pulls back his head a bit. "She's just doing what she thinks is right."

"No, she's doing what she feels like. What she wants. But there are more people involved than just her and her whims."

"She's not your mom."

"What? That's not …" And fine, maybe some of my own issues have bled into this conversation, but why am I suddenly the enemy here? I press my thumb against my lips before I say anything else I might regret.

"Sorry, Ken. I don't mean to fight." And the man just looks so forlorn as he pushes a hand through his curls, bringing them into disarray. "I just don't see a way around this. The girls are my first priority."

His words sink deep into my soul.

The girls …

Not me.

And I'm not saying that I *should* be his first priority. We're too new. And the girls depend on him. But doesn't he see? "Ryan, you cannot give and give to other people without finding a way to refill your own tank. You need people supporting you as well. And you have friends, co-workers here … you have me." It sounds a lot more whiny, more pathetic, out loud than it did in my head. "You have to take care of yourself in order to take care of them."

"But how? I can't ask you to move with me, Ken."

The air whooshes from my lungs. How did I not consider that possibility? I open my mouth to tell him I *would* move—but the words won't come.

Why won't they come?

He continues as if my brain hadn't just exploded. "You love it here. And you're starting school soon—I know you'll get in. You've got your life on track." He tilts his head and looks at me with so much love, I think it might be melting my inner core. "And I still wonder if you shouldn't tell your grandma you'll go work for her. Like I'm stopping you from getting your inheritance. I know you say I'm not, but I can't help but wonder … if you and I weren't together …"

"Do you really think that?"

I said no to her for my own reasons. It didn't really have to do with him. Did it? If Ryan didn't exist, if he and I hadn't found this beautiful connection, would I be in San Francisco right now? Crap. I don't know. I don't think so.

But I can't say for sure.

Ugh, I'm so confused. But I need to get this conversation back on track. Back to the logical. "Ryan, we're talking in hypotheticals here. Your sister might make a thousand different decisions between now and then."

"But if she does decide to move, I have to go with her."

Why does he keep saying that? "No, you don't." I sigh. "But we can deal with that when we get there, okay?"

"I can't do that to you," he whispers. "I can't ask you

to give me the next three months, knowing that we might have to end things when Sophie gets out of jail."

Wait, what? "What are you saying?" A pause. "Are you … breaking up with me?" Before we've even had a real chance?

The silence of this moment between us stretches until it's so thin, it's bound to break any second. And it's like cotton is stuffed in my ears, because I hear nothing but the hissing of my own blood as it races through my veins.

Ryan removes his arm from my shoulder. Turns his head away from me. "I think that might be best."

"But … but what about the girls? My job?"

"Of course you still have it, if you want it. But if you decide that it's too much … I'll understand if you quit."

Oh, screw this. I stand up. "I don't quit on the people I *love*."

The bold declaration hangs between us. He realizes I'm talking about him too, doesn't he? *Look at me. Look at me*, I silently command.

But he doesn't. He just leans his head into his hands balanced on his lap. "I'll do my best to stay out of your way at home, then."

Seriously? Is this all the response I'm going to get from him? But he's just sitting there, frozen. Quiet.

"Don't bother. I'm moving back in with my sister." Hopefully Alexis will be okay with that. "You can just text me your schedule each week and we'll figure out how to best *avoid* each other."

Are we really doing this? Ending things because his sister *might* need him to move? I know he's doing what he thinks is right. What he thinks he must. The worst part is, I can't even be truly mad about it, because I know it's motivated by his love for his nieces. As much as I don't agree with his decision, I admire him for it.

Honestly, it only makes me love him more.

Which is why, when I walk away from him into the happy carnival crowd, I feel like my insides are splitting in half. My heart has finally stalled on the hillside, and it's drifting backward, down, down, down.

About to crash into a thousand pieces.

eighteen

. . .

THE LAST WEEK and a half has been a whirlwind of spring break activities with the girls. Of tears. Of moving all of my stuff back to Alexis's and fielding questions from my young charges—though Ava just looks at me with sad eyes, like she knows what's going on.

That one is wise beyond her years. And I hate that for her.

But the reality is, I can only do so much for them since I'm just going to be in their lives for another two and a half months. Their mom has already spoken with them about making the move to Oklahoma. As expected, Ava hates the idea and Mila doesn't care so long as they get their mommy back.

Whenever I think about it, I nearly throw up.

I feel that way a lot these days—especially when I think about Ryan. About what we had. What we lost.

What *he* ended for the both of us.

"Argh." I wrestle with the tape on a closed box of cupcakes from the bakery that provides Java Awakening with our pastries. We're out of them in the display case up front and Josh sent me back to the kitchen to get more. But obviously this bakery likes to use industrial-grade tape to secure their boxes, because I can't get the stupid stuff off. "This is ridiculous." Marching to the counter beside the fridge in the back area, I snag a huge chef's knife off the wall. It's possible I have a maniacal look in my eye as I turn back to my quarry and raise the knife like a half-crazed hunter.

"Whoa there, mate." A flash of blonde in the corner of my vision distracts me momentarily, and then Chloe is there, her hands raised as she approaches me like I'm a toddler wielding a blowtorch. "Put down the knife and no one needs to get hurt."

"Ha ha." I slash through the tape on the cupcake box and pull it open. Ah. Victory at last, in some part of my life.

I'm pathetic, I know.

I glance around, but it's just Chloe, dressed fashion-ably as usual in a belted long-sleeved jumpsuit, her hair in ringlets that cascade down her shoulders. "Where's your guard dog?"

"Tia had a family emergency. Got called away this morning." Chloe plops down on a stool at the island and reaches for a cupcake.

I swat her hand playfully, a move for which I would have either been sufficiently rewarded with Tia's narrowed eyes or a takedown I wouldn't see coming. "A bit of freedom, then?" Pulling loose the chocolate cupcake she was eyeing, I set it on a napkin and scoot it across the granite countertop toward her.

"Until my father and brother send someone new. I'll probably get stuck with some old fuddy-duddy who's worse than Tia. But it's glorious in the meantime. Nobody watching my every move for no reason."

"To be fair, there *is* a reason." My mouth quirks up—the first smile I've worn in days. "You *are* a freaking princess."

"As true as that might be, I'm not in any danger here. We're not like the Windsors. Most Americans don't even know where Kentonia is, much less who I am."

"Still. I'm sure Topher just wants you to be safe." It feels good to speak about—to think about—something other than my sadness. I lift out another cupcake, place it on a second napkin, then take the box with the rest of the dozen in hand. "I'm just going to take these to Josh."

Biting into her cupcake, she closes her eyes and waves me off. I hurry up to the front and carefully move the individual cupcakes inside the display case before dusting off my hands and asking Josh if I can take my break. With only a few patrons seated in the shop and nobody in line, the mid-morning Monday rush has definitely ended. Should be another hour until things pick up for lunchtime.

"Yeah, of course." He gestures around. "We're in a lull, as you can see."

"Thanks. Just let me know if you need me." I head back through the swinging kitchen door and lean over the counter across from Chloe. "So, how was your trip?"

She, Lauren, and Shelby left the day after the

carnival and just returned late last night from a week in Hallmark Beach, the adorable town between Los Angeles and San Francisco where Shelby and Eric will be getting married in July.

"It was great. We met several times with the wedding planner, stayed at the most charming little inn, and took some time to relax." Chloe takes a lick of frosting from the top of her cupcake, then sighs. "I did feel a bit sorry for Lauren, though. Shelby has the freedom to make her own choices about what she wants for her wedding. And Lauren is stuck with Flutterbum and all her ideas that don't say anything about Topher and Lauren themselves except that they're royal. It's complete rubbish."

I unwrap my adorable cupcake, with its pink frosting and two cut halves of sliced strawberries arranged to resemble a heart. "If only they could be like Jim and Pam on that old show, *The Office*—"

"Whoa there. Watch what you're calling old." Her blue eyes sparkling, Chloe winks at me. "You might just be inadvertently calling your friends old as well."

The remark is innocent enough, but reminds me of Ryan, and I can almost hear the word *Young'un* float from his lips through my mind. Blowing out a breath, I shake off the ghost of the memories, refocus on Chloe. "Anyway"—I look at her pointedly—"they knew that everyone at their workplace was going to make their wedding about themselves, so they snuck away and got married privately beforehand." My thumb swipes some frosting that I stick in my mouth. The sugar is a shot of joy that disappears just as quickly as it arrives. "It's a shame something like that isn't possible."

Chloe sets down her cupcake and stares at me. "You're a genius, Ken."

"What do you mean?"

"Ah! I can't believe I didn't think of that. What if … no, I can't get ahead of myself. I'll need to talk to Topher first." She claps her hands and releases a very undignified squeal. "This could be amazing."

"You'll have to let me know what you're thinking when you get it figured out."

"Of course." Chloe stands as if to leave, then blinks and sits again. "Sorry, that's not why I came to see you. I wanted to see how you're doing."

I shrug and shove a bite of cupcake into my mouth. "I'm fine," I mumble, some crumbs falling out. Ugh, is this how low I've sunk? Standing, I walk to the fridge and grab a few water bottles, hand one to Chloe, and twist off the cap to wash down this pastry—and my utter humiliation.

Because I really thought that Ryan was the one.

To have failed at a relationship again … and so soon after Brooks … double ugh.

Chloe's face softens. "You're not fine. I'm sorry we haven't been able to talk through it all until now. Though I *did* try to call." She trails off.

"I know." But I didn't feel like answering. Didn't feel like explaining to anyone, even Alexis, who was surprised to see me back at the house but didn't dare say *I told you so*. Instead, she just held me and asked whether she needed to murder Ryan or at the very least slash his tires. I love her, but didn't want her overreacting, so just said we mutually agreed to go our separate ways except for reverting back to being boss and employee. Ones who saw each other as little as possible.

But it's been a very lonely nine days, and Chloe's always steered me right in the past. Maybe she can help me see what went wrong. So I push aside the rest of my cupcake and tell my friend everything. Outside this room, the coffee grinder whirs, patrons chatter, music plays. But in here, I fully recount the breaking of my heart out loud for the first time since it happened.

When I'm finished, Chloe snatches up my hand and gives it a good squeeze. "Aw, Ken. I'm so sorry."

I sniffle. "Thanks."

"But …"

"What?"

She studies me. "Well, if you love him as much as I suspect you do"—Chloe pauses, waits for me to protest, but I've got nothing. Because she's right. I love Dr. Ryan Freaking Rosche and there's no coming back from that.

"That's what I thought. So if you love him, then why didn't you tell him you'd move with him anywhere he went?"

My mouth falls open. "He didn't ask."

"Of course not. The poor man is probably worried that you'll either reject him by saying no, or that you'll regret it and change your mind if you say yes."

Like Jillian did. "You think that's why he brought up me going to San Francisco again?" Even though the subject was closed in my mind.

"That would make sense to me."

Releasing Chloe's hand, I stand and pace, tugging at my hair. "This is all so dumb. His sister will probably get out of jail and change her mind. Or, sadly, relapse."

"So then why not go to him, tell him you want to stay together? To see where things go?"

"He didn't give me that option, Chlo."

"Since when do you need permission?" Chloe straightens and shakes her head—and in this moment, with that determined set to her jaw, the princess emerges. She's positively regal. "You've been afraid since the day I met you, but it's time to fight for what you want, Kennedy. Show Ryan that you aren't giving up on him. That you're not leaving."

Something thrums in my blood at the idea. But … "I didn't leave. *He* quit on me! Just like Brooks. Just like Mom. Just like my grandmother, who hasn't spoken to me since I didn't give her what she wanted. Why am I never enough, Chloe?" And there it is—the full truth. My chest heaves, constricts, the pain of the confession sitting there, making it hard to breathe. "I *know* Ryan's not like any of them." My voice trembles and I slump with my back against the counter, sliding to the floor. "But I just can't help but feel like I'm not enough for *him* either."

Chloe joins me on the cold tile, taking my hand in hers again. "Nobody who has seen you together can doubt that he loves you too."

Oh, my heart. *Does* he love me? That almost makes this worse. Was our love not enough?

My friend continues. "It sounds to me like Ryan is used to sacrificing what he really wants for the greater good. For the good of those he loves. Ken, don't you see? He loves you so much that he let you go."

Tears are falling onto my jeans now and I swipe at them. My fingers come away black from my smeared mascara. Can what she's saying be really true? When I think about the look in his eyes the night of the carnival, before his sister's call, I can see it—the fact that he thought we were headed for forever too.

I blow out a shaky breath. "But what if I do change my entire life for him? What if I *do* leave Alexis and all of my friends here behind, ditch my schooling, and follow him to Oklahoma—and then he dumps me again?"

"I know that's a scary possibility. But the reality is that you can go to school to become a social worker anywhere, including Oklahoma. And Alexis might very well move away someday to be with Dax. You just never know what the future holds. All you can do is live for today." Chloe pushes her hair behind her ear. "Because what if you *don't* break up? What if you get married and have babies and all of your dreams come true? That's just as likely a scenario."

"Not if you look at my past."

"Our past doesn't dictate our future, Kennedy. Only we can do that, if we're brave enough to speak up and take what we want." And there she goes with that far-off look in her eyes again, making me wonder if she's thinking of what *she* really wants. "So if you push all of your fears aside, what *is* it you want? And what will you regret more in twenty years—going after it and possibly being rejected, or not going after it in the first place?"

It doesn't take me long to decide what I'd regret more.

Still, I'm an adult now. Instead of running off, I have to finish what I started, and that includes my work shift. But my hands itch as I serve up coffee after coffee, as I toast bagel sandwiches and greet customers and try not to let my jitters show.

I glance at the clock for the hundredth time. Ugh, why am I torturing myself like this? I don't get off for another hour, and thirty minutes after that, I'm due to pick up Mila from school. Ryan's at work all day and overnight, and Mila's home tomorrow when he finally gets back. So most likely, I won't get a chance to talk with Ryan tonight at all.

Chill out, Kennedy. This is not the end of the world. But now that I've made the decision, the idea of waiting another day—another second, really—to tell him feels impossible.

And yet. I must.

But that's where working for a friend comes in really handy. Because when the lunch rush finally dies down, Josh faces me, leaning back against the counter. "You seem a bit off. Everything okay?"

"Just got a lot on my mind."

"I hear that." Josh tugs at the corner of his beanie.

"One of those things wouldn't happen to be Ryan, would it? Kayla seems to think …" He shakes his head. "Never mind."

"Kayla's probably correct." Wiping my hands down my apron, I blurt out the unfortunate truth. "I need to make things right between us."

His chin tilts up, eyes open with understanding. "Well, then what are you still doing here?"

It takes me a second to get his meaning. But once I do, I squeeze his arm in thanks, hang up my apron, and hurry outta there with my purse like there's a sale at my favorite store. I don't even know if Ryan will be available to talk, but maybe there's a small chance.

And I'm desperate enough to go full throttle after that chance.

When I exit the coffee shop, droplets of rain find my bare arms. I don't even bother to snag my sweater from my purse, because I'll be in my car in a minute anyway, but brrr. The sun has gone into hiding. This morning, that perfectly reflected my mood. Now, though? I'd give anything to see a few rays of light—of hope—breaking through the clouds.

Once I'm in my car, I speed like a mad woman toward Ryan's hospital. I briefly contemplate driving right up to the emergency department doors, but figure that I should probably leave the space clear for actual emergencies even though this definitely feels like an emergency of the heart. Unfortunately, that means I have to park in a garage and of course the only free spot is on the very top level. Then it takes five full minutes of walk-running in the rain to get to the ER. Hopefully nobody cares that my clothes are wet. At least I wore jeans, a black (not white!) blouse, and canvas tennis shoes, so I'm able to move fairly quickly.

I enter the building and a cold artificial breeze at the door tackles my hair. The ER isn't overly crowded, so I'm able to get to the reception desk in seconds. An elderly woman with bleach-blonde hair smiles up at me. Her red, glitter-painted glasses wink at me. "How can I help you, hon? You need to check in?"

"No." Though I'm sure I look ill, with how I'm doubled over breathing hard, my hair plastered to my cheeks, which are probably bright red. "I'm actually here to see one of your doctors. Ryan Rosche?"

"Ah, Dr. Rosche. Nicest man ever, isn't he?" She smiles and clucks. "But he doesn't take appointments, sweetheart. He just works in our emergency department."

"No, that's not …" I close my eyes because the room has started to spin. That can't be good. Then again, all I've eaten today is half of a cupcake. "I really need to see him. Can I just go back there?"

Her expression shifts into something narrower, less open. Is she suspicious of me? I should explain that I'm his girlfriend—or was, anyway. But at the moment, my ears are buzzing, and some black spots dance on the edge of my vision. My stomach feels like it might expel something. "I'm sorry, I just need a minute." I bend in half, put my hands on my knees. The woman says something to me, but I don't hear what.

Before I know what's happening, someone—maybe

a nurse?—is helping me into a wheelchair. "Put your head between your legs, sweetie."

Oh no. This is not what I had planned at all. But considering the way my body is acting, I do as she asks. She strokes my back as I take deep breaths. Eventually, the light-headed feeling passes and I sit up. "I'm so sorry," I whisper.

"No need to be sorry. Why don't we take you back and get you checked out?"

"Oh, that's not necessary. I'm just here to see—"

"Dr. Rosche. I heard." The forty-something nurse, whose scrubs are covered in Sesame Street characters, pushes a button and rolls me through a set of double doors that open automatically. "Have you seen him here before? He's one of our best doctors. Nobody cares more about his patients than Dr. Rosche."

Am I surprised that Ryan has charmed his co-workers and patients as much as he has charmed me? Nope.

The nurse wheels me into a partitioned bay surrounded by a curtain, then covers my shoulders with a scratchy hospital blanket, gets me up on the edge of the bed, and takes my vitals. She's quick, efficient. And it's all happening so fast.

"Ma'am, this is all a misunderstanding." I try to get my fuzzy brain to work. "I think my blood sugar was just low and then I ran here and it was raining and I didn't drink enough water today—"

"Don't worry, sweetie. We'll get you all fixed up." Then the nurse starts asking me a series of questions and I answer them as best I can. But when she hands me a fresh hospital gown to change into, I realize this has gotten way out of control. I don't have money to pay for a hospital visit, and even if I did, I just need to see Ryan.

That's *all* I need.

"I'm sorry, I don't think this was a good idea." I stand up. "I've got to go."

"Oh sweetie, I don't recommend that. You could faint again."

I take a step and teeter a bit. Sheesh. My blood sugar isn't playing games, is it? "I'm just here to see Ryan."

Her eyebrow quirks, maybe at my familiar use of his name. She gently takes my shoulders and steers me back to the bed. "All right, if I go get him right now, will you stay put?"

Biting my lip, I nod, then climb onto the bed once again. The nurse lowers it back a bit before ducking out around the curtain. I settle against the pillow and close my eyes, try to steady my breathing, my heart.

I'm about to see Ryan again. I might be pale, wet, and hungry, but this is me. Kennedy, the hot mess. He can take me or leave me, but not until I say my piece.

The curtain rattles open then closes again, and I hear his quick intake of breath—a near-silent gasp. Then, "Kennedy?"

I open my eyes to the most beautiful sight in the world. The man I love is standing over me, the lower half of his face covered by a surgical mask, his eyes filled with concern.

"Are you okay?" He holds up a clipboard. "It says here that you nearly fainted in the lobby." Ryan grabs my hand and presses his fingers to my wrist. Can he feel it when my pulse kicks up a notch?

"I'm fine. Just some low blood sugar and maybe dehydration after running here." The tension is so thick that I kind of wish I had that chef's knife from earlier to slice through it. Maybe a joke will do it. "Though actually, maybe I could use some CPR."

His brow furrows. "You're breathing just fine."

Okay, then. Score one for the awkward silence.

Ryan drops my hand and steps away. "I think we should run some tests on you. Get some fluids going." Why has he gone all clinical on me? Retreated into his shell?

Because he doesn't know why you're here, you idiot.

Right. Leaning forward, I snatch at his scrubs, catching the edge of his shirt before he gets too far away. "I don't think I need all that."

His mask may be obscuring his mouth—that beautiful mouth—but I can still see his Adam's apple. It bobs at my statement. "And what do you need?"

I smile and tilt my head. "Well, let's review the facts, shall we? I got off work early and instead of going home, I came here. Then there was no close parking, so I literally ran to the ER." Giving his shirt a tug, I lean forward. "And you know how much I hate to run."

"I do." Slowly, he sets the clipboard down at my feet and removes his mask. It's probably good that he wears that thing in here—otherwise, many more patients would be having heart attacks at the mere sight of his strong jaw, that stubble, those all-too-kissable lips.

As for me, it's like a shot of adrenaline to my tired brain, bringing everything into focus.

"So what was so important that you had to do the thing you hate most in the world?"

"I decided that I had to run after what I want." I pat the spot next to me. "And that's you, Old Man."

He sits beside me on the edge of the bed. His left hand rests on my thigh. There's a sheen in his eyes, tears that aren't falling, but that serve to brighten his gaze on me. "I want you too, Young'un. That's not the issue."

"Ryan, I'm not Jillian. And you're not Brooks. Neither one of us is in a power position here. Neither of us gets to make decisions for the other one. We should make decisions together. If it comes to it, and *we* feel like we need to move to Oklahoma to support Sophie and the girls, that's a decision we'll *both* make." I run the tips of my fingers over his knuckles, up and down each finger. His shudder tells me all I need to know about whether he's as affected by my touch as I am by his. "I … I love you, and I don't care what might or might not happen. We can face that together. Whatever comes." I inhale through my tears. "Love is a choice, and I choose you, Old Man. I choose you now, and I'll choose you then. Just give me a chance."

He scoots closer to me, his arm moving around my back, my waist. "You love me?"

"More than anything."

Ryan puts his forehead against mine, but instead of closing his eyes, he keeps watching me. "I love you too, Kennedy. I'm sorry if you thought my actions indicated that I didn't. If my ending things was me trying to be in control. I was just trying to protect you. Protect the girls. Protect everyone. But you're right, as usual. If I've learned anything in the last week and a half, it's that I can't do this alone. I need help to help them. I need you." He kisses me just under my eye, and his lips come away wet with my tears. "I just don't want you to regret this."

"By *this*, do you mean a man who loves me so much he's willing to let me go? A connection like I've never known before in my life? Someone to watch *The Bachelor* with me every night? A hot doctor whose impeccable good looks are only second to his amazingly big heart? Ryan, how could I ever regret choosing that?"

He coughs, his cheeks red. "I don't deserve you, Young'un." Then he buries his face in my neck, and I throw my arms around him, holding him tight.

"Yes, you do. You deserve all the good things."

"And you are definitely that," he whispers into my skin before setting it on fire with his kiss. His mouth moves from my neck up to claim my mouth, and I surrender.

Over and over and over again.

Finally, I collapse back onto the bed with a happy sigh. "I guess I should let you get back to your doctorly duties, hmm?"

"And you should get back to your nanny ones." He taps his watch. "Mila gets out soon. But are you sure you don't want me to give you a more thorough exam?"

I waggle my eyebrows. "Well ..."

The tips of his ears turn pink. "You're terrible."

"You love it," I tease.

"I love *you*." He says it so sweetly, so solemnly, and I don't think I'll ever get tired of hearing it. Which is how I know that I'm going to marry this man. I don't know when. I don't know how. I don't know where.

But those things aren't important. The important things are the who (Dr. Ryan) and the what (being there together through thick and thin) and the why (because he makes me a better version of myself).

And the fact that together, with hard work and commitment to our love, we can conquer anything.

epilogue

. . .

Seven Years Later

TODAY IS both a beginning and an end.

The end has been coming for a while, bit by bit, a slow detaching and turning of the pages of time. But as hard as the end is, the beginning is just as sweet.

Even sweeter, given the surprise Ryan and I have for everyone.

"You look beautiful, babe." I sneak up on Ava, where she's staring at herself in her bedroom's long mirror.

"You think?" She tugs at the thin straps of the dress we went shopping for together a few weeks ago. It's modest but stylish, flaring out a little above her knees, a white lace overlay covering the pink material underneath. Her blonde hair is styled in an adorable pixie that suits her quite well, as does the tiny nose ring piercing she got on her eighteenth birthday. Ryan wasn't too sure about it—went on about how dirty so many of those piercing places are—but I just teased my husband about being an old man and that shut him up right quick.

Or maybe he shut *me* up with kisses. Yeah, that was probably it.

"I do think. And I'm sure Joseph will think so too," I tease.

She narrows her eyes at me through the mirror. "He might not even show up."

Stepping forward, I hug her from behind, gathering her in my arms like she's my own. Well, technically, she is—Ryan and I adopted her and Mila five and a half years ago, after Sophie decided she couldn't care for them like they deserved and left in the middle of the night with only a note. Kayla introduced us to an amazing adoption attorney who was able to track down Sophie and the girls' dad for signatures so we could adopt them without any issues.

That was *also* the end of something. But oh, what a beautiful beginning it was. Just like Ava's graduation earlier this week. And tonight, at the party we're throwing her. All of our friends have come back into town to celebrate it—the first of our kids to graduate is kind of a big deal—and it's going to be loud and crazy.

This might be my only chance to have Ava alone.

"If he doesn't, it's his loss. But who wouldn't want to attend the party of Point Loma High's gorgeous valedictorian who was admitted to multiple Ivy League schools? He'd be an idiot to not show up, if you ask me."

That gets an eye roll, and an affectionate smile and pat. "Thanks, Aunt Kennedy. At least I have you in my corner."

"Always." And grab a paddle, folks, because the

river of waterworks has begun and they're threatening to last a while. I stare at this girl who has become a beautiful and responsible young woman—there were moments in her teen years when Ryan and I doubted it would happen, but it did—and I am overcome with gratitude. That I was granted the opportunity to be a mom to her, especially when we couldn't …

I bite my lip, remembering my secret. My unbelievable secret.

"You're gonna make me ruin my makeup," Ava complains, pulling away and twisting to face me. "Let's get out there and stuff our faces with chocolate! You did say there would be chocolate, right?"

"Duh. Uncle Connor has been baking and cooking up a storm." Blowing out a breath, I place my hands around my neck and unclasp the cross necklace I always wear. "But I wanted to give you something before we got this party started."

Her eyes well up and she shakes her head as I hold the necklace up to her throat. "You can't give me your mom's necklace. It's the only thing you have from her."

"That's not true." While I thought that at one time, I know better now. "I have all my memories of her, good and bad. All the things she taught me, whether she meant to or not."

"Still." Her lip trembles. "You should save it in case you …" Ava looks away. "In case you ever have a daughter of your own."

"Hey, now." I shake the necklace at her and she turns back to me. "You and Mila might not be my blood, but you're both the daughters of my heart."

Once I secure the necklace around her throat and she turns to stare at it in the mirror, then we're both crying and hugging each other and our mascara has to be fixed. It's a good ten minutes until I'm ready to meet and greet everyone who has probably arrived at the shindig that stretches between our unfenced backyard and that of Shelby and Eric—who bought Alexis's house from her when she quit her job, started up her own freelance design business, and moved to Los Angeles shortly after Shelby and Eric got married.

"Knock knock."

I recognize that voice anywhere—even after seven years, I still hear it in my dreams every night—and turn to find my handsome doctor standing at the door. His hair is still curly, though a bit shorter, and he's wearing jeans and a button-up blue shirt that matches his eyes. The sleeves are rolled to reveal his muscular forearms, which are basically works of art I could admire for hours. "Hey," I say.

"What's all the crying for?" He turns his attention to Ava and whistles. "Well, if it isn't the prettiest eighteen-year-old in the world."

Ava walks up to him, lifts on her tiptoes, and kisses his cheek. "Thanks, Uncle Ryan."

"Are we ready to go out?" Tomboy Mila bounds into the room, her cheeks slightly dirty and her hair yanked back in a ponytail. Hard to believe this eleven-year-old who wears baggy jeans and oversized T-shirts is the same girl who played with dolls incessantly and rarely wanted to wear anything but a princess dress when she was four. But she's still full of the same energy, the same joy, and that's all that matters.

"Yes, yes, let's go. I think Auntie Alexis is on greeting duty." At eight months pregnant, it's the only thing she really *can* do.

Mila puts on a fake grimace. "Do you think that's a good idea? She might scare everyone away."

We all laugh at the truth in that statement, especially since pregnancy has brought out the harsher parts of her personality. The only things that calm her down are a Marvel movie marathon and Dax. (Though if you ask Alexis, this whole situation is his fault since he got her pregnant in the first place. I like to remind her it takes two to tango. That always makes Dax grin in that way that drives my sister nuts.)

Ava loops her arm through Mila's and they march down the hallway. Ryan pins me with that look—the one he's been giving me every day since we met in one way or another. He leans down and kisses me, but instead of the heated passion I've come to know, it's soft and gentle. He's handling me like I'm porcelain these days—afraid I'll break.

I get that, but it also drives me up a wall sometimes.

"Let's go, huh?"

"You sure you're feeling up for this?" he asks quietly. "We don't have to tell anyone just yet."

I move my hand from the top of my stomach to the bottom. "I'm seventeen weeks. People are gonna start to notice soon." But I understand his hesitancy. After two losses and then nothing for three years, we've both been afraid that spilling the beans will somehow jinx things.

But I don't want to hide our joy anymore. I want to hope for better things. And I know that the people who have mourned with us over our pain will celebrate with us too. Because that's what family does— and those people out there are my family. Much more than Gran, who hasn't spoken a word to me since I turned down her offer to work at Montgomery Inc. Not even when I got married to a freaking doctor. Or graduated with a master's in social work. Or started working at a reputable agency as a family support specialist.

But the family outside? They're the ones I know will never leave. Who come back together for the important events like this one.

Ryan grabs my hand and pulls me through the doorway of Ava's room, down the hallway, past the living room where I fell on him years ago, and out the back door into the late afternoon sun. The warmth of June has brought sunny skies and longer days. Finley rushes to greet us, though how he hears us over all the ruckus is a wonder. There are children EVERYWHERE —and it's no surprise, given that there are fourteen kids among our friends (and that's without counting the babies inside of Alexis, me, and Lauren). Once he sees that we're good, Finley races off in pursuit of one of Josh and Kayla's five children, two-year-old Cassian, who is toddling around with a slice of bacon. Easy pickings, that.

Ava's standing on the grass talking to a boy who can only be Joseph. I elbow Ryan and glance that way. "Look."

He frowns. "Do I need to be concerned about something?"

"Stop it. You'll embarrass her, Old Man."

His frown turns upside down. "Well, that *is* my right as the father figure in her life."

I giggle as he lumbers across the yard, clapping his hand on the guy's shoulder. Ava's eyes go wide and find me. I just wave and shrug.

Alexis waddles over from the spot near the back gate. "Who's the guy?" She fans her face with her hand. It's not that hot out but she *does* have a little heater inside her.

"Joseph," I say, as if that explains everything. Then I arch an eyebrow at her. "Aren't you supposed to be sitting down and greeting people?"

"Yeah, well, as you can see, my charming husband has taken over that job."

Oh yes, I do see. I snort at the sight of Dax telling a story with big sweeping motions to Eric, Topher, and Chloe's husband. I need to get over there at some point and ask Topher how kingly life is treating him. We all attended his coronation but it's been a year and a half, and though I've had a chance to talk with Lauren, Topher's been understandably busy.

"Who is Ava talking to?" Evie wanders over to join us, holding five-year-old Jane's hand. Jane's got a big smudge of mud on her cheek but is as adorable and bright-eyed as ever. Before now, I haven't seen the little girl since Evie and Connor moved to Iowa three or so years ago after Evie's dad had another heart attack. Since Connor's romance novels make them a boatload of money, and Evie's job let her go remote, they help manage the work on Evie's family dairy farm. Evie says it's a great place to raise her two kids, and that having the kids around is a wonderful way to help keep her parents young. "And what's Ryan saying?"

"I was wondering the same thing." Kayla does lunge squats across the yard. How does the woman even do that with a six-month-old strapped to her chest? Then again, she's always been a beast—building a business of ten dating coaches from scratch while popping out baby after baby (and one set of twins, named Luke and Ben). I don't know how she does it, except that Josh obviously helps. In fact, just a few years ago, he turned over management of Java Awakening to a co-worker, Hannah, and went full-time as a stay-at-home dad. The role fits him quite perfectly. "Do you think she might be interested in my services?"

Alexis groans. "She's eighteen."

"So? It's never too early to learn how to have self-confidence. That's really what I teach the most, you know."

Evie snickers. "Yes, some of us know allllll about the power poses."

Kayla's hand lands on her hip. "Well, they work, don't they? And I'll have you know that my advice landed each and every one of you a husband." She turns her nose in the air. "What an ungrateful lot."

"Who's ungrateful?" Shelby pops into the circle. Chloe is close on her heels.

"All of you. Well, maybe not you." Kayla pats Shelby's shoulder. "You know the value of the advice I give."

"What, to just haul off and kiss a guy if you can't figure out what else to do or how you feel?" Lauren joins in the fun, holding her toddler on one hip. James Theodore (or JT for short—yes, in a roundabout way, she named her child after Justin Timberlake) is curled up, asleep on her shoulder, his left leg looped over and supported by her rounded belly.

We all laugh, even as Kayla sputters. "I'll have you know I charge a hefty fee these days for my advice. You all were lucky early guinea pigs."

"No one was more of a guinea pig than your own husband," Evie teases. "I still love seeing how far you've come. From the woman who thought she'd never marry to a mom of five kids—"

"In my defense, I only wanted two. But that man is just too darn sexy." Kayla finds Josh across the yard, where he's throwing back a beer with Kevin, Connor's brother from NYC who took the opportunity to visit Connor and his dad, who lives up in Los Angeles. His wife Lola, a big-time Broadway costume designer, is here somewhere in the chaos with their two kiddos.

As if he can sense Kayla talking about him, Josh looks up and lifts his eyebrows. She blows him a kiss. "I just can't say no to him. Thus, this." She points at the baby snuggled against her chest.

"Girl, I feel that so hard." Alexis grimaces and grunts, one hand on her stomach. Another Braxton Hicks? A part of me hopes she ends up having the baby down here so I get immediate auntie privileges. Not that

that would be much fun for her. But I'm still so afraid she'll have a fast labor and that I'll miss the birth. "Pregnancy sucks."

Then her eyes flit to Shelby, then Chloe, then me, and she pales. "I mean …"

"Don't look at me," Chloe says, hands raised. "We still don't even know if we want kids." She and her husband have spent much of the last few years traveling and settling into their careers.

"Okay." Alexis snags her red braid and pulls it around to the front of her shoulders. Gives Shelby and me another once over. "But—"

"It's okay, Alexis." Shelby smiles in that way she has, where all her sweetness shines through. "We weren't all meant to have biological children." She and Eric actually tried a few rounds of IVF using her sister Deb's eggs, but they didn't take. "But I feel really blessed to have the kids we do. They needed us, and we needed them. Even Eric believes things have turned out exactly as they were meant to and doesn't have any regrets." They adopted two nine-year-olds a few years back, and have their home open to new foster kids too. It's pretty incredible, really. They've already touched the lives of over twenty kids who have been in and out of their home.

And then I feel everyone's eyes on me—and not their pity, exactly, but their sympathy. They know how much I've longed to give my husband a child, despite all the love I've poured into Ava and Mila over the years.

"Excuse me for a minute, okay?" I walk away, but can feel their gazes. They probably think I'm sad, that

I'm stepping away because I can't stand the topic of pregnancy anymore.

And maybe that's been true in the past. But I've come a long way. Actually, even before the stick told me that there was life inside of me, I had come to a place of peace with our situation.

And then, the most incredible gift. One I'm terrified to lose.

But Chloe said it best all those years ago—*"You just never know what the future holds. All you can do is live for today."* And I intend to.

I approach Ryan, who has moved on from Ava and Joseph (much to Ava's obvious delight—the girl's a smitten kitten) and is standing with Connor at the grill. When I reach him, I stand on my tiptoes to whisper in his ear. "It's time."

"Yeah?"

"Mmm hmm."

He takes my hand and kisses it, then turns to Connor. "Sorry, man. I'll be back to hear more about that."

"No problem, dude." Connor flips a burger. "Take your time."

Hand in hand, my husband and I walk to the center of the grassy area, and we turn to face our friends—our family. "Hey, guys. Can I have your attention for a moment?" Ryan says.

After a few moments and an ear-splitting whistle courtesy of my sister, everyone quiets. Even the kids seem to know something big is about to go down.

"Thanks to everyone for coming out to celebrate our amazing Ava."

Across the lawn, Ava gives a little wave then ducks her head. My gaze roams the rest of the yard, connecting with each and every person's I can see, stopping on Alexis's. Her eyes are scrunched in scrutiny, looking at me like she knows something's up. Guess I shouldn't be surprised. Sisters always know.

Ryan squeezes my hand and smiles down at me. Oh, how I love this man. Oh, how I love this life. And it's only getting better. We're not losing. We're gaining. With each day, each new life, each tragedy, and each triumph.

The end of one thing—and the beginning of another.

"And we don't want to take away from that celebration. But there's something more …" My husband clears his throat and places a hand on my stomach. "We have an announcement to make."

And the crowd goes wild.

Ahhhhh! I can't even believe that this is the end of the California Dreamin' series. I've had soooo much fun bringing these characters to life, and I hope you've enjoyed the journey as well. Like Kennedy said, though —this is the end of one thing, and the beginning of another.

Because here comes a brand-new series!

If you want to see Princess Chloe get her happy

ending AND meet the charming (and hilariously quirky) people of Hallmark Beach, then check out *Beachside Kisses With My Bodyguard* (coming soon). You'll get to catch up with old friends and meet new ones.

But first, I can't let this series go without adding a fun little extra for you. If you want to read the scene where Kennedy runs into Dr. Ryan in her towel—this time from *his* point of view—then head to kristincanary.com/neighbor and subscribe for a peek into his thoughts.

books by kristin canary

California Dreamin' Series

Enamoring Her Amnesic Ex (prequel)

Loving the Ladies' Man

Desiring His Dating Coach

Saving the Secret Prince

Belonging With Her Best Friend

Engaging the Office Enemy

Needing the Next-Door Neighbor

Hallmark Beach Series

Beachside Kisses With My Bodyguard

about the author

Kristin is a wife and boy mom who functions best on peach tea and cookie dough ice cream. A desert dweller, she always has her eye on the next trip to a beach somewhere—and if she can't travel there in person, then you'd better believe she's going to write about it. Kristin is never fully satisfied with a movie, TV show, or book without a hefty dose of romance in it, and she's grateful to be living a true-life love story with her own crazy little family. Connect with her at KristinCanary.com.

facebook.com/kristincanary

instagram.com/kristincanaryauthor

www.ingramcontent.com/pod-product-compliance
Lightning Source LLC
Chambersburg PA
CBHW061614190726

48288CB00007B/2322